MW00912323

Barnabas
Bigfoot
A CLOSE SHAVE

To Robert -

MARTY CHAN

Watch out for the "squatch"

thistledown press

© Marty Chan, 2011
All rights reserved

No part of this publication may be reproduced or transmitted in any form or by any means, graphic, electronic or mechanical, including photocopying, recording, or any information storage and retrieval system, without permission in writing from the publisher or a licence from The Canadian Copyright Licensing Agency (Access Copyright). For an Access Copyright licence, visit www.accesscopyright.ca or call toll free to 1-800-893-5777.

Thistledown Press Ltd.
118 20th Street West
Saskatoon, SK S7M 0W6

Library and Archives Canada Cataloguing in Publication

Chan, Marty
Barnabas Bigfoot : a close shave / Marty Chan.
(The Barnabas Bigfoot series ; bk. 1)

ISBN 978-1-897235-92-8

I. Title. II. Series: Chan, Marty. Barnabas Bigfoot series ; bk. 1.
PS8555.H39244B37 2011 jC813'.54 C2011-905352-7

Cover illustration by Derek Mah
Book design by Jackie Forrie
Printed and bound in Canada

We acknowledge the support of the Canada Council for the Arts, the Saskatchewan Arts Board, and the Government of Canada through the Canada Book Fund for our publishing program.

A big hairy hug to James Tapankov & the tech challenge students in the Pembina Hills District for giving me the story starters.

A hairy hug to Jackie Forrie, Diane Tucker, Derek Mah, Corinne Chan, Father Jan School, Belmont Elementary School, Lise Henderson, Michelle Chan, Marissa Kochanski, Wei Wong.

The biggest hairy hug of all to the Alberta Foundation for the Arts for their support of this book.

CHAPTER ONE

When your family name was Bigfoot, size mattered. My ancestors were proud of their name, but they were even more proud of their massive feet. Etchings of my great, great, great grandparents and their gigantic feet filled the rocky walls of our cave home: my great, great, great uncle Boondoggle picked fungi from between his massive toes; great aunt Brunhilda balanced a boulder on top of her hairy foot. On the cave roof was the largest etching: Grandma Bertha doing a double kick, lifting her huge feet so high they were level with her bushy eyebrows. The pictures invited the next Bigfoot to join them on the cave's walls. Every Bigfoot could claim to have the largest feet in the tribe. Every Bigfoot, that is, except me.

Everything else about me was completely normal. I stood seven feet tall, a little above average for a sasquatchewinian boy of twelve winters. Long soft brown hair covered every single part of my body like moss on the shady side of a stone. I knew how to blend in with the surrounding fir trees and disappear from sight, a survival skill every sasquatch needed against the baldfaces who camped at the bottom of our mountain home. I could disappear better than any other sasquatch in the tribe, so quickly that you'd think I was a ghost, but while I was the best at hiding myself, I couldn't hide my tiny feet from my curious tribe members.

Jackrabbits had long ears. Moose had huge antlers. Sasquatches had large feet. Our tribe believed in the power of the foot so much that the sasquatch with the largest pods always served as tribe leader. Grandma Bertha had a saying: "You'd better have big feet to follow in the footsteps of the leaders who walked before you." She had led the tribe for many winters, just as her father had ruled and now just as my mother did. Grandma Bertha had high hopes that I'd be the next tribe leader.

When I was eye high to a hairball, she squeezed my foot and told me stories about her dad protecting our mountain home against a wandering grizzly bear. She claimed he kicked the angry bear off the mountain with his giant tootsies and that after that, no bears ever bothered us again. This kind of courage ran in the Bigfoot family. Mom had travelled to a faraway mountain to save our distant cousins, the Yeti clan, who were separated from our tribe and lost in a snowstorm. I couldn't wait for my feet to grow, so I could take my rightful place as leader and set off to do hairy deeds that would become well-groomed tribe legend.

When my eleventh winter passed, I began to bloom. Every sasquatchewinian child longed for the blooming, because it meant they could finally set off into the woods without asking for permission or having an older sister go with them. Like every other sasquatchewinian kid, the hair on my chest sprouted from a bald patch to a lush meadow. I grew tall and straight like the mighty mountain pines near our cave home. My hairy hands grew as large as beaver tails and my scrawny arms and legs became as thick as tree trunks. The only things that didn't grow were my feet.

My parents told me I was a late bloomer and not to worry, but Grandma Bertha treated me differently. Instead of squeezing my feet, she started to pull on my toes and told Mom to keep me in the cave until my tiny tootsies grew. She didn't want the other sasquatches to see me, arguing that our tribe survived because we learned to avoid anything that was odd or out of place. Different meant dangerous. A grizzly bear was different. A mountain lion was different. My small feet were different. Grandma Bertha said she didn't want my feet to scare the others.

But I knew the truth: she was disappointed in me. Her dreams of another Bigfoot taking over the tribe and carrying on the family tradition had shriveled like a dried blueberry. While she didn't say it aloud, I could see her bushy eyebrows droop as she stroked her beard and glanced sideways at my feet. She was right about keeping me away from the others. Sasquatchlings would tease me as soon as they saw my tiny feet. They'd cough up hairballs of sloppy nicknames: Barnabas, the tiny terror,

Tippy Toes Barnabas, Littlefoot, Pine Cone Toes, Small-squash. Sasquatchlings could be very cruel. I agreed to stay inside the cave until my feet grew, but Mom wouldn't hear of it. She said she was proud of me because the size of my heart made up for the size of my feet.

Mom and Grandma Bertha argued about what to do. If I hadn't been so upset about my feet, I would have found it funny to see my mother argue with Grandma Bertha the same way I argued with Mom.

"Barnabas is staying in the cave," Grandma Bertha stated.

"He's going out," Mom argued.

"Don't you take that tone with me, young sasquatch."

"But, but, but . . ."

"No buts, Bernice Belinda Bigfoot."

"It's not fair, Mom."

"That's the way it has to be."

At one point in the argument, it looked like Mom was holding her breath to get her way. Grandma Bertha had a way of turning my mom — the tribe leader — into a sasquatchling. In the end it was my dad who unknotted the mat of our hairy problem: he made a disguise for my feet.

At the foot of my bedrock sat two hairy things that looked like bird nests that would cover what Grandma Bertha called my "special condition." I didn't like wearing them, because they made my feet itch, but Grandma Bertha insisted that I wear them whenever I left the cave.

"Barnabas," yelled Dad from outside my rocky room. "Wake up."

"I'm up, Dad!" I yelled.

"Time to forage for leaves. Are you ready?"

"Almost."

"Do you need help?"

"Dad, I'm twelve winters old. I can do it myself," I shouted. "I'm not a little kid."

"Don't take that tone with me, Barnabas Bonner Bigfoot."

"Sorry, Dad!" I yelled, then I muttered to myself, "Saying my full name isn't going to make me move any faster."

"I heard that!"

I climbed out of my bedrock, but as soon as my feet touched the ground I started to topple over. My hands shot out and caught the wall in time to avoid a full-on face plant. The problem with my puny feet was keeping my balance, especially when I tried to stand up too fast. Instead, I sat back down on the bedrock and crawled across the stony surface to grab my fake sasquatch feet.

Dad made the fake fuzzies from a pair of foot-hides Mom had found near a baldface shelter. The baldfaces were the gruesome hairless creatures who sometimes camped near the base of our mountain. These beasts covered their ugly hairless bodies with bright-coloured hides, including the foot-hides my mother had found among the garbage the baldfaces had left behind. They were wasteful beasts, tossing old food away and leaving behind their possessions when they migrated south. Often we'd find their garbage and tried to make use of it so as not to let anything go to waste.

White strings crisscrossed the top of the foot-hides and strange etchings covered the gummy soles. These things were so big I had to stuff leaves inside to keep my feet from slipping out. Even the puny baldfaces had bigger feet than me. Grandma Bertha had a saying: "The hungry crow can't complain when there are only slugs to eat." Either I could let everyone in the tribe see my small feet, or I could wear these things until my feet grew.

The good news was that the foot-hides not only hid the ugly truth about my feet, but they also gave my feet a wide enough base that I didn't topple over every time I stood up. Dad had covered the foot-hides with his own hair so they looked like regular feet. As long as no one looked too closely, the fake pods seemed real. The only problem was the trail they left behind. The foot-hides made weird zigzag patterns in the dirt. I had to shuffle when I walked to erase the patterns, which made for very slow moving. I was always the last one out of a cave, last one to climb up a tree and last one to jump in the lake. The sasquatchewinian kids called me "Snail-Squatch" to my face. I could only imagine what they called me behind my hairy back.

"Hurry up! The Hairysons are waiting for us," Dad yelled.

"I'm putting on my feet now," I said.

My fake left foot was a bit loose, but as long as I didn't run the foot-hide would hold. I walked outside and spotted Dad and Mom talking to Juniper Hairyson, one of the nicest sasquatches in the tribe. She always gave me the first pick of blueberries when she came back from harvest and she never had a mean word for anyone, which was why I was so surprised her daughters turned out to be so cruel. Ruth and Hannah Hairyson pelted me with rotten blueberries whenever I wasn't looking, and they were the ones who came up with my nickname, "Snail-Squatch."

Grandma Bertha had a saying: "You can't tell if it's day, unless you have night." Everything in nature had an opposite. For day, there was night. For fire, there was water. For sky, there was land. For the sweet Juniper Hairyson, there were two sour daughters.

Ruth and Hannah were mountains of mischief not just for me, but for every sasquatchewinian kid. A few moons ago, they bugged some girls who rubbed hairy honeysuckle under their arms to smell fresh. The sisters badgered the sasquatchlings mercilessly, claiming the honeysuckle attracted cougars. They claimed smart sasquatches smelled like bear droppings, because the harsh scent kept cougars away; dead sasquatches smelled like honeysuckle. Since then, every sasquatchling rolled around in bear droppings, more likely to keep safe from the Hairysons' teasing than from prowling cougars.

Hannah was forever curious about anything to do with baldfaces. Every summer night, the furry blonde sasquatch spied on them at the base of the mountain. Mom warned that if the baldfaces found out where we lived, they'd probably round us all up and throw us in cages like their tiny fluffy dogs that yipped and yapped. Hannah claimed she was learning about baldfaces to protect us, but I think she secretly liked them.

On the other hand, Ruth liked making fun of me and she made no secret of it. When she discovered that the hair on my cheeks curled into ringlets whenever I was embarrassed, she wouldn't stop teasing me. She called me names. She made me the butt of her jokes. She found a head full of hairy ways to embarrass me.

Watching the dark-furred Ruth whisper to Hannah now, I knew she was plotting to curl my beard again. As long as Mom stood nearby, I was safe. No one ever dared to cause any trouble around the tribe leader. I lumbered to my parents and Juniper Hairyson. I wanted to stick to Mom like honey to fur.

Ruth Hairyson cut me off at the pass and cracked a crooked yellow smile. "Hey, Mom, don't Hannah and Barnabas make a sweet sasquatchewinian couple?"

My cheek hair curled so tightly that it looked like my face had broken out in pine cones. I shuddered to think what Ruth would do if she ever learned about my small feet.

Juniper Hairyson shook her head. "Hairball, you know better than to tease Barnabas."

She plucked at my curly beard. "Don't have a hairy, Mom. He doesn't mind. Do you?"

I said nothing, glaring at her as I batted her hand away.

She smirked. "Besides, I think Hannah is tied up in knots over him."

Hannah flashed me a smile, flashing her dingy buck teeth. A stringy, half-chewed leaf dangled from between her front teeth. She twirled a finger around it and winked at me. I felt hairy tornadoes whipping up all over my beard.

"Look, he feels the same way about her," Ruth said. "Isn't that hair-dorable?"

I looked at Mom, hoping our tribe leader would put her foot down and end the sisters' pesty plucking. Instead, my mother nudged Dad. He chuckled as if he had just heard a good joke.

"Say, I have an idea," said Ruth. "Can Hannah and I go with Barnabas to forage for leaves this morning?"

Mom nodded. "Of course."

Juniper Hairyson warned, "Don't go near the baldface camp."

Hannah smiled. "You know us, mommy."

"My dad needs help picking berries," I said.

"Barnabas, are you a Snivel-Squatch," Hannah whispered. That was her insult for whiners.

Hannah was trying to goad me, but I wasn't going to fall for her trick. Nothing was going to move me from my spot.

"Go with the girls," Dad insisted.

"Yes," Mom agreed. "It'll be fun."

"Hairy armpits!?!" I screamed. "Why are you making me do this?"

"Groom your hair, Barnabas," Dad said. He wanted me to relax, but there was no way

I could, knowing that I'd be alone with the Hairyson sisters.

Mom brought up one of Grandma Bertha's sayings: "A chick that never leaves the nest will never learn to fly."

"Spread your wings, little chickie," Hannah giggled.

Dad scooped up two sticks of celery from Mom's gathering basket, tied them together with strands of his hair, and tossed them to me. "You can share a snack with the girls."

"Forget it," I said.

"Don't you take that tone with your father, Barnabas Bonner Bigfoot."

"But, but, but . . . "

"No buts," Mom interrupted.

"This isn't fair," I mumbled.

"That's the way it has to be. Go with the Hairysons," she ordered.

Ruth grabbed one of my hands, while Hannah took the other, and they dragged me into the woods. I dug my heels into the dirt, but sasquatchewinian girls were stronger than boys. The sisters yanked me down the trail and into the woods.

Behind us I could hear Mom telling Juniper Hairyson, "Ruth is right. I think Hannah and Barnabas make a hair-dorable couple."

My cheek hair curled again, so tight my cheeks hurt.

CHAPTER TWO

As the Hairysons led me deeper into the forest, my nose twitched from the scents of our forest home. The earthy moss. The herbal fir trees. The sweet hint of ripe berries. We were getting close to the berry bushes, but Ruth veered to the right, cleared away some brush and headed down a new trail. She motioned for us to follow.

"You're going the wrong way," I said. "The bushes are this way."

Ruth twisted her moustache and cracked a wicked smile. "Well smell a skunk and call it sweet, Barnabas can tell directions."

"Where are we going?"

Hannah shushed me. "It's a secret."

She pushed me ahead of her. As we stumbled down the steep trail, I hoped my fake feet would stay in place. I glanced at the celery stalks dangling around my neck and wondered if this was Dad's idea of finding me a girlfriend. Grandpa Benson had told me how his mother hung vegetables around his neck so he could make new friends. Friends like Ruth and Hannah, I didn't need.

The trail soon flattened out and the loose dirt gave way to hard-packed ground, made uneven by the odd tree root here and there. Ruth hiked through the heavy forest. Hannah stayed behind me, nudging me forward when I slowed down. As we walked down the slope, the smells changed. The fresh scent of pine and moss turned to something bitter. There was the strong hint of rotting food, as if a sasquatch had forgotten her winter stores and left them out under the sweltering sun for far too long.

"We're near the baldfaces," I said.

Ruth turned and beamed. "Who wants to play Baldface Chase?"

"What are you talking about?" I asked. "We're supposed to stay away from these creatures."

"Shhhh," Hannah hissed.

"I'm going back home," I said.

"Don't be a Scaredy-Squatch, Barnabas," said Ruth. "This will be fun."

Hannah played with the rat tail she had braided out of the hair on the back of her neck. "Come on. Aren't you even a little bit curious about what baldfaces do?"

As much as I hated to admit it, I was. These creatures always left a huge mess whenever they came to the mountains. Some destroyed trees. Others killed deer. One tried to kill the lake with some foul black liquid. If Grandma Bertha's saying about day and night was true, the opposite of nature was a baldface. The more we knew about these hairless beasts, the better chance we might have of surviving in spite of them.

"Lead the way," I said.

Hannah knelt down and crawled through the brush. The soles of her hairy feet were matted with dirt and leaves. Ruth waved me to go next, but I couldn't let her see the soles of my feet.

"You first. I ate beets for breakfast," I said as I waved my hand behind my butt.

Ruth scrunched up her nose and went down on her hands and knees. I followed, glad the

Hairyson sisters weren't going to see my fake foot-hides. The scent of the baldfaces' shelters grew stronger as we moved through the brush. They smelled like dead lilacs and burnt leaves. Last winter, our tribe had to clear out the baldfaces' camp because the smell was so bad. That's where Mom found my foot-hides. I had always wondered why these creatures were so messy; now I was about to find out.

Hannah stopped at the trunk of a wide tree and slithered up the bark until she stood upright. She waved at us to stay low. I peered through the brush and spied on the baldfaces' camp.

A female baldface lumbered out of a massive white boulder. This monstrosity looked like a snow-covered rock formation that had been carved into the shape of a giant sharp-edged log. The boulder sat on black circles and had a clear-ice front that allowed us to look in and the baldfaces to look out. Dad called these boulders rolling caves, because they could move and they seemed to be where the baldfaces slept.

The female baldface with blue hides on her legs and a red and black hide over her body raised a tiny silver box to her face and aimed it at the male one next to the fire. The box gave off a blinding flash.

"Hairy armpits, what is that?" I asked.

Hannah said, "Groom your hair. It can't hurt you. I call it an instant etcher. The baldfaces use it to draw pictures. I think that flash burns the etching all at once on a little icy section on the back."

I gave Hannah a puzzled look. Just how much time had she spent around the baldfaces?

She grinned sheepishly. "I found one of the instant etchers last summer. A baldface must have dropped it. It worked for a while, but then the etching went black. I tried shaking it out, but nothing happened."

Ruth added, "They're such curious creatures. If they weren't so short, they could be our hairless cousins."

She was right. Other than their height and lack of hair, the baldfaces looked just like us, but they didn't act like us. Their machines fouled the air. While a sasquatch left a footprint, baldfaces left garbage. If we were distant cousins, we definitely did not learn the same manners toward nature.

"Do you think we might be related?" I asked.

Ruth shrugged. "Maybe."

"Quiet," Hannah whispered. "It's time. Sweet cherries, this is where the fun begins." She began to move forward.

"I get to go first," Ruth said, pulling her sister back.

Hannah shook her blond hair. "You got to go first last time. It's my turn."

"I called it first."

"I said I'd do it last night," Hannah argued.

The sisters kept at their hairy fit until I silenced them both with a sharp hiss. "The baldfaces will hear."

Ruth nodded. "Barnabas is right. Besides, it's not fair that we drag our new friend all this way and not let him go first."

"Fine," Hannah said. "Barnabas, you have the honour of going first in Baldface Chase."

"Thanks," I said. "But it'd mean a lot more to me if I knew what Baldface Chase was."

She explained, "It's a game. We score a point for every baldface who chases us. The sasquatch with the most points wins the game."

Baldface Chase sounded reckless.

"Forget it," I said. "This is like when you made Dophelia Longlockson play Wake the

Black and White Cat." A few moons earlier, they had teased Dophelia about being scared of animals. They'd tricked her into petting a sleeping black "cat", which turned out to be a skunk. To this day Dophelia still smelled rank.

Hannah beamed. "You heard him, Ruth. He's too much of a Scaredy-Squatch to go. I get his turn."

Ruth growled at her sister. "Fine. Barnabas, you have to pick the winner. Careful. She cheats."

"Do not," Hannah said as she straightened up. She walked along the edge of the tree line, crunching through the fallen leaves and swinging her long arms against the branches. Her rat tail of hair swished from the back of her neck. The crashing sounds soon attracted the baldface trying to build the fire. He stood up and pulled off the green hide covering his head, revealing a few grey hairs on the balding top.

Ruth tugged on my arm. "He has to chase after her. She'll say that standing up counts, but it doesn't."

Now I knew why they wanted me to come along. They needed a tiebreaker for their arguments.

Hannah rushed back. “One point for me.”

“He didn’t chase you,” I said.

Ruth beamed.

Hannah growled. “Ruth’s been talking to you about the rules, hasn’t she?”

I shook my head. “If the game is called Baldface Chase, the baldface really should chase you.”

She folded her hairy arms and scowled. “You think it’s easy getting them to come after you?”

“Doesn’t look that hard,” I lied.

Hannah’s moustache drooped and her shoulders sagged as she pouted. I owed her for coming up with my nickname.

“If you think it’s so easy, why don’t you try it?” Hannah taunted.

Ruth waved her sister away. “He’s a judge. Besides, it’s my turn.”

Hannah sneered. “Scaredy-Squatch is hiding behind Rutabaga Head.”

“Well, well, well, look who climbed up a fir tree and says she’s above the rest of us,” Ruth said.

"Look who's throwing a hairy fit because she knows I can beat her."

"Oh yeah?"

"Yeah."

The sisters moved toward each other, the hair on their backs stiffened so high that it looked like porcupines had jumped on for a ride. I slipped between them.

"Enough," I said. "If you can't make one baldface chase you, Hannah, don't blame me for it."

Ruth chuckled. "He got you good."

Hannah's beard bristled as she glared at me. "Why don't you try it if you think it's so easy?"

I don't know why, but I liked being the itch under Hannah's fur. "Sure. I'll give it a go."

She grinned. "Fur-tastic."

Ruth stood up and smoothed the hair on her arm. "I'll be the judge. Barnabas, all you have to do is get them to chase you. If you get one, great. Two is even better. The record for a chase is 300 strides, but you won't beat it."

"He will," Hannah said. "She doesn't want you to because it's her record."

"Stuff a hairball in that cave you call a mouth," Ruth said.

“Okay,” I said. “I’m ready.”

“Good luck,” she barked as she shoved me forward.

Hannah had made the mistake of walking along the tree line to get the baldfaces’ attention. Sasquatches were best at blending in, so all the baldfaces heard were some weird noises. If they were going to chase anything, they’d have to have more reason than some rustling.

I walked away from the trees and headed for the two creatures. I groomed my hair, calming myself as I waited for the pair to look my way. The one crouched over the fire dropped his stick and stared at me. His female partner stepped back and let out a short scream. I ignored them and veered to the right, walking back into the woods where I knew I could blend in.

Behind me, one of them yelled, “George, get the camera!”

I didn’t know what a camera was, but I hoped it wasn’t a weapon. I picked up the pace just in case it was. I wanted the baldfaces to chase me, not hunt me. As I reached the safety of the trees, I groomed my arm hair which was standing on end. Behind me, footsteps. The chase was on.

I didn't need to look back, because the dead lilac scent of the baldface filled my nose. The stronger the scent, the closer the baldface. I strained to hear the footsteps behind me. More than one. I had attracted *both* baldfaces. Hannah was probably gnawing on her big foot right about now.

Then I heard a loud click, which was followed by a bright flash. I walked faster, aiming for some large trees where I could disappear. I wasn't about to let the baldfaces get any nearer. I counted off my strides. Two-hundred and fifty seven . . . eight . . . nine . . . sixty . . . sixty-one . . . By the time I was deep into the woods, I was at 288 strides. Twelve more and I'd match Ruth's record. Thirteen more and I'd have bragging rights.

I peeked back. The baldfaces had stopped. The female one held up a silver box and pointed it around the woods.

"There he is," yelled her male friend. "Shoot him."

Shoot!? Forget the record; I had to save my hairy butt. I loped into the woods trying to get away from the baldfaces. They crashed through the woods behind me, but they weren't going to follow where I was going. I waded into a soupy bog.

Behind me, I heard shouts of dismay as the baldfaces stumbled into the deep swamp. I smiled. Their legs weren't long enough to stride through the muck. I waded to the other end of the bog, and then doubled back to Ruth and Hannah's hiding spot. I spied the helpless baldfaces trying to back out of the bog and yelling at each other. Maybe this could be a new game. How many baldfaces could a sasquatch lead into a bog?

As I walked back to the sisters' hiding place, I expected Hannah to crown me champion, which would come along with all the joy of never having to be teased by the Hairyson sisters ever again. I couldn't wait to see the look on Ruth's bearded face as I told her how many strides I had walked. I wanted to tell them both about how easy it was to set a new record, but there was only one thing that kept me from enjoying my sweet victory.

The sisters were gone!

Chapter Three

I felt like a strand of hair jammed in an eyeball: unwanted. I kicked myself for falling for the sisters' hairy-brained scheme. They were probably having a good chuckle up on the mountain. The Hairysons' prank didn't have a hair out of place. I couldn't tell Mom what they did, or else I'd get in trouble for visiting the baldfaces. I didn't know how or when, but some way I was going to get even with Ruth and Hannah.

A distant bang startled me. Someone was coming out of the baldfaces' rolling cave. Not just someone — Hannah. She carried a small brown bag. She peeked around the site and then waved back at the giant rolling cave. Ruth stepped out, holding a little golden bag. She said something to her sister. I couldn't hear what they were saying, but I knew they were stealing.

I rushed toward them. As soon as they spotted me, they hid their bags behind their backs. I sniffed the air, hoping to smell what they had stolen. It was something sweet. Not quite like honey, but close. Then another scent drifted up my nose. Less sweet. More bitter. Almost like roasted bark. Together, the two smells made my mouth water.

"What do you think you were doing?" I demanded.

Hannah glanced around. "Are the baldfaces still chasing you?"

I shook my head. "They're stuck in a bog. It'll be a few breaths before they get here. Are you stealing from them?"

The sisters said nothing, but their ear hair spoke volumes. Whenever they lied, their ear hair flapped like a bird's wings. If Ruth and Hannah's hair flapped any harder, they'd be lifting off the ground.

"Put the bags back," I said.

"We're always picking up their garbage and using it," Ruth said.

Her sister added, "What's to say they're not going to throw this out anyway?"

"Because they haven't thrown it out yet. You two should be ashamed of yourselves."

"The baldfaces steal from us all the time," Hannah said. "They never ask if the berry patch belongs to anyone. They just pick all the best blueberries for themselves."

Ruth backed up her sister. "Don't you remember when the baldfaces came through last snowfall and chopped down the pine tree?"

A tribe of baldfaces had marched into the forest and cut down a pine tree that had been home to a chipmunk family for many winters. The chipmunks lost their entire winter food stores. I fed them the scraps of food that Mom and Dad foraged until the snow melted. It had been a very hard winter for the chipmunks. Three of the youngest ones died.

"Two cracked branches don't make a tree," I said, reminding the sisters of the old sasquatch saying about revenge. "Now put back whatever it is you stole."

As the tribe leader's son, my word could leave deep footprints. One word to my mother could turn the sisters into the rotten berries of the entire tribe. Hannah's moustache sagged, while Ruth pulled the bag out from behind her back. As soon as she did, the bitter roasted bark smell punched up my nose and nearly bowled me over. Hannah opened her bag and the sweet scent drew me near.

"What's in the bags, anyway?" I asked, pretending not to care.

Hannah opened her sack. "This is sweet sand," she said. "It's the best thing you've ever tasted."

Inside were white sand crystals that smelled sweeter than any beehive I had ever come across. Ruth waved her golden bag under my nose. A roasted bark scent filled my nostrils and sent shivers up my spine. The brown powder in that bag looked like fresh soil that had been ground fine.

Ruth said, "I don't know what the baldfaces call this stuff, but I like to think of it as delicious dirt. Smell."

I shrugged.

"Tastes even better with the sweet sand," Hannah said.

She claimed they had found other bags of the baldface food last summer when they were cleaning up a baldface camp. The Hairyson sisters had found all kinds of food in the mess, from orange bark chips that tasted like sasquatch sweat to puffy white snowballs that never melted. Among the food they found was some sweet sand and delicious dirt, which Hannah claimed could be put together to create a bittersweet treat.

"Do you want to try some?" Ruth asked.

I shook my head.

"Just a taste. Don't be a Scaredy-Squatch." Ruth pushed the bag toward me.

The strong smell drew me forward, but I wasn't going to fall for any more Hairyson hijinks. I pushed the bag away.

"When my mom finds out, you two are going to be in so much trouble," I said.

"Snitch-Squatch," Ruth hissed.

"Sour berries!" Hannah screamed.

I looked around the woods, half expecting the baldfaces with their camera weapon to fire on us. I ducked low, but in the clearing there was nowhere to hide except maybe under the rolling cave. No baldfaces were in sight. Instead, Hannah pointed down at my feet.

"What the tangle is that?" she screeched.

Ruth looked down at my feet. "Great mossy rock, that is disgusting."

I peeked down. My fake feet had been soaked in the bog, and the fur clumped together to reveal the white foot-hides underneath. My feet looked like they had been boiled to the bone.

"W-w-what happened to your feet?" Hannah asked.

"Nothing."

"Hold your hair! Those aren't his feet. He's wearing baldface foot-hides," Ruth accused. "Look."

I stepped away before Ruth could grab my foot-hides. If problems were trees, I was in the middle of a dense forest. There was no way the sisters would forget what they saw. They pelted me with questions, one after the other: "What's wrong with your feet, Barnabas? Why are you wearing foot-hides? Can we see your feet? Why won't you show us? Why can you steal baldface things and we can't? Does your mom know?"

I refused to answer any of their questions, but the sisters kept at me like a father plucking ticks from his sasquatchling's head. I shuffled away, wishing I had never gone along with them in the first place.

"Show us the foot-hides," Ruth begged.

"Please. I want to try them on."

"No."

I walked toward the woods, trying to get away. The sisters stuck to me like thistledown burrs on my hairy legs, pleading with me to show them my foot-hides.

"Why do you wear the foot-hides?" Hannah asked.

"None of your business," I said.

Ruth guessed, "I bet he's one of those baldface-lovers. I heard about sasquatches like that. Remember the story about Furdinand Flatfoot's great uncle? They said he shaved off all his hair and went to live in the baldface world."

Hannah turned to me. "Baldface Barnabas."

"You're one to talk. What would your mother say if she found out you were stealing from the baldfaces?"

"She won't find out." She raised herself to her full height and stared down at me. "Isn't that right, Baldface Barnabas?"

I backed up a few steps and bumped into Ruth. My forest of trouble seemed pretty thick right about now, almost as thick as Ruth's hairy arms that had wrapped around me in a sasquatch squeeze. I struggled to get free, but sasquatchewinian girls were naturally stronger than boys. While sasquatchewinian males cleaned caves and cooked, the females gathered wood and cleared rocks, which meant they had to climb trees to snap off branches and carry huge bundles on their broad backs. This helped them build up their upper body strength. At her young age, Ruth already had powerful arms that she used to crush me.

Hannah ran her fingers through my beard, grabbed a handful and began to twist. Pain shot through my chin and cheeks.

"Hairy armpits, that hurts!" I yelped.

"Now let's see what's so special about the baldface foot-hides," Hannah said.

I squirmed helplessly in the grip of Ruth's powerful arms. If the sisters saw my tiny feet, there was no way I could stop them from spreading the word to everyone in the tribe. Not only would I become the bald patch of the tribe, but the other sasquatches might question my mother's right to lead the tribe. There was only one way to stop the Hairysons.

"As the tribe leader's son, I have to report everything I see and hear to my mom," I said. "Normally, that's what I'd do, but there's a hair out of place in this situation."

Hannah stopped. Ruth relaxed her grip. I had their attention, and I wasn't about to let up.

"Grandma Bertha has a saying: two robins might not get along, but they'll still build a nest quicker together."

Ruth let go of me, while Hannah eyed me up and down. I hoped they would accept my offer to protect our secrets.

Hannah spoke first. "If we don't say anything about your foot-hides, you're willing to forget about the sweet sand and delicious dirt?"

I nodded. "But you have to Sasquatch-Swear to it."

Hannah looked over my shoulder at her sister. They didn't say a word to each other, but their fluffy beards said it all. Ruth glared at her sister, while Hannah rolled her eyes. Then they had a staring contest that lasted about fifty breaths. Hannah seemed to win. Ruth refused to budge, the hair on her back and shoulders bristling as her sister turned to face me.

"You go first, Barnabas," Hannah growled.

I nodded. Then I plucked a hair from my chin. No sasquatch would freely give up their hair unless they were serious about making a promise.

"I Sasquatch-Swear never to say anything about you taking the sweet sand or the delicious dirt," I said as I held up my loose strand of hair.

Hannah and Ruth smiled, flashing their crooked yellow teeth. Hannah elbowed Ruth, who glared at her sister and shook her head. Hannah sighed, then she reached up to her chin and yanked out a hair. She let out a yelp. She held up her strand of hair.

"I Sasquatch-Swear never to say anything about your foot-hides," she promised.

I nodded.

Hannah barked at Ruth, "Do it."

"Fine, fine." She made the Sasquatch-Swear with a long brown strand from her beard.

Our deal was sealed by the hair on our chinny-chin chins.

Chapter Four

As soon as we reached our cave homes, the Hairysons split away from me faster than a coyote skittering away from an angry bear. The sisters had tied their baldface bags together with strands of Ruth's long, brown back hair, then hung them from a tall branch in a fir tree many strides from our home. They didn't care that I knew their hiding place, because our Sasquatch-Swear kept me from telling anyone.

Hannah eyed my foot-hides as she walked away. I wondered if she wanted the foot-hides for herself and moved away quickly. I wished I had never gone foraging with the sisters. Grandma Bertha said, "A hair pulled out can never return. All you can do is wait for a new hair to take its place." I hoped I'd find another solution to this hairy knot of a problem. For now, I would avoid the sisters.

At dinner, Dad served mushy yams with dried leaves. The orange dish looked pretty on the blue plates some baldfaces had thrown out last summer. The baldfaces never seemed to keep anything. Either they were very forgetful about their belongings, or they didn't care about what they owned. We had to clean up after them. Better not to waste anything, we used their leftovers rather than let them collect mold and dust in the woods.

Mom wolfed down her dinner, placed her big feet on the rock table, stuck her whiskers into her mouth. She chewed them thoughtfully as she laced her hands behind her head.

"So, Barnabas. How was foraging?" she asked.

I shrugged. "The Hairysons spent more time fooling around than looking for berries. That's why we came back with so little. Sorry."

"I noticed you didn't share the celery with anyone," she said. "Maybe you'll have a chance tomorrow when you go out with the sisters again."

Dad scratched his dark brown chest hair and shook his head. "Leave the matchmaking to me, Furball. You have enough going on with running the tribe."

Mom fixed a hard look at Dad. He shook his head and cleared the table. She lifted her feet off the table and leaned forward. Her deep brown eyes were like twin owl eyes hunting for a mouse. I flinched from her gaze, afraid she'd swoop down on me. She smiled, flashing her dingy yellow teeth.

"Look, Barnabas. Hannah has really big feet. There's a good chance she could run the tribe. It'd be nice to keep it in the family."

"My feet may still grow," I said. "I could still become the tribe leader."

She smiled, "Barnabas, have you ever heard Grandma Bertha's saying about winter? You can always count on it to come, but you can't count on when. Better for us to prepare now in case it shows up early or, in our case, late."

Dad picked up the last of the blue plates. "Furball, did you hear about the Yetis? They're expecting another sasquatchling next spring. We should send Yolanda Yeti some roots to make some tea. Maybe we could walk over tonight."

"Are you trying to change the subject, Bartholomew Bigfoot?" Mom asked.

He chuckled. "You can always smell my little schemes."

Mom laughed. "Okay, I get the point. Barnabas, you can go foraging by yourself tomorrow. Unless you want company."

"He'll be okay on his own," Dad said. "There's a time to wash and a time to scrub."

This was his way of telling Mom she was trying too hard. She sighed. "You're right."

Mom might have been the leader of the tribe, but when it came to me, Dad knew what to do and say. She backed off for now.

"Dad, do you need help cleaning?" I asked, eager for the chance to get away from Mom.

He tossed me one of the plates. I scooped some sand on to the blue plate and scrubbed off the caked-on yams.

"Maybe later we can play star shapes," he suggested. "Furball, do you want to join us?"

Mom's heavy snoring gave us her answer. She sounded like a bull moose during mating season. I glanced at Dad and snickered. He raised a yam-covered finger to his lips and shushed me, but his moustache curled with his glee.

Later, while Mom unleashed a snore storm in the cave, we stepped out. We climbed the steep slope near the caves, moving away from the cluster of pine trees that sheltered us from the baldfaces. As we climbed higher, the air grew colder and thinner. The pine smell faded away. Above the cave was where I felt like I belonged. Sometimes, I wondered if I wasn't meant to be a hawk or an eagle.

We reached the familiar flat rocky ledge that was the best spot for star shapes. The ledge gave us a fur-tastic view of the mountain range and the cloudless night sky. Dad took my hand and swung me over a wide gap and on to the ledge. My foot-hides skidded across the loose pebbles.

He jumped on to the ledge behind me. His feet gripped the rock, keeping him from sliding. Sasquatch feet weren't just big; they were also as sticky as spider webs. Sasquatches could clutch anything with their feet. Well, not every sasquatch; only the ones who didn't have to hide their embarrassingly tiny feet inside fake foot-hides.

Up here, no one cared about what I wore. It was just my dad and me sitting on a rocky ledge and playing star shapes. He plopped down beside me and pointed to a group of stars in the northern part of the sky.

"That looks like a good place to start," he said.

"Sure," I said, beaming. "I'm ready."

"Let's see, let's see. Okay, I've got one. Follow my nose to the horizon until you see the largest star. Climb the vine of stars until you see the red star. Then hug the four stars on either side. What do you have?"

I looked where Dad's nose was pointing and followed an invisible line over the mountains, where I spotted a giant star. This had to be the one. I squinted hard to make out the shape. The only thing I could picture was the rat tail of hair that hung off the back of Hannah's neck.

"Is it an animal?" I asked.

"Ah, you think it has a tail," Dad said. "But what looks like a tail to you, might be something different to me. Brush the stray hairs out of your mind."

I looked at the night sky again, trying to let the stars shape into something, but I couldn't get past the twinkling tail and the thought of Hannah becoming my mate. Was Mom insane? I was thinking so hard I think I started a fire in my brain.

"Groom your hair, Barnabas," Dad said. "Don't force your shape to fit the answer you want. Let the shape come to you."

Again, I tried to make out the figure. "It's a raccoon. No, a coyote. No, a snake that just ate a mouse. Is it a rat tail?"

Dad laughed. "Sometimes the easiest ones are the toughest. Do me one thing, Barnabas. Close your eyes."

I did. The night sky disappeared.

"What do you see?" he asked.

"Nothing."

"Really? Not even the inside of your eyelids?"

I smiled. "Okay, yes, the inside of my eyelids, but they look like nothing." I felt a tapping against my eyelid.

Dad said, "Doesn't feel like nothing."

I smiled. He always had a way of seeing things differently than everyone else. Maybe that's why he wasn't so upset when he found out that I had small feet. Instead, he hugged me and told me I had the most amazing feet in the forest.

"Barnabas, are you asleep?" Dad started to tickle the hair under my armpit.

I laughed. "I'm awake. I'm awake."

"Just checking. Now tell me what the inside of your eyelids really look like."

"They're black. Like the night sky without any stars or moon," I answered.

"Good job. That sounds like the inside of your eyelids. Now open your eyes and look at the vine of stars and tell me what you see."

I looked at the vine of stars. They didn't look so much like a tail this time. Instead, they looked more like a vine; something thin to hold up a cup of stars. Not a vine. A stem.

"It's a dandelion," I yipped.

Dad ruffled the hair on my head and beamed. "Neat nose hair, you're getting good at this game."

"Can we go again?" I asked.

He smiled. "As many tries as you want."

We played star shapes until Dad told me he was running out of night sky, but I asked him to find more shapes. I never wanted the game to end, but my body had another idea. My arms grew heavy. My head started to bob up and down. My eyelids started to droop. I rested my head on my dad's furry shoulder. Any thought of twinkly stars or Hannah's rat tail started to fade away with every yawn. Before I knew it, I was staring at the inside of my eyelids and nothing else.

Chapter Five

Eight sunrises had been and gone since the Hairyson sisters and I made our Sasquatch-Swear. I tried to stay away from them, but Mom kept braiding Hannah and me together. Mom gave me a bunch of celery and hinted that I should ask Hannah to go on a picnic. When I refused, she asked Juniper Hairyson if Hannah wouldn't mind going for a walk with me. The strange thing was, Hannah didn't seem to mind hanging out with me. In fact, she was eager. Too eager.

"Don't worry, Bernice Bigfoot, I'll take good care of Barnabas," Hannah said sweetly as she took my hand and led me away from my meddling mother.

Once we were in the woods and away from prying eyes, the Hairyson sister shoved my hand away and turned on me.

"I want to try on the foot-hides," she demanded.

"Hairy armpits!? What?"

"Give them to me."

I should have been relieved that she didn't want to pluck at me again, but instead I felt let down.

"Forget it, Hannah. You'll break them with your big feet." Her pods were like a duck's webbed feet, if the duck were the size of a grizzly bear.

"Good sasquatches are supposed to share," Hannah said. "You've been wearing those foot-hides so long, I think you're starting to act like one of the selfish baldfaces."

"Says the sasquatch who is hiding sweet sand and delicious dirt from everyone in the tribe," I shot back.

She pulled her rat tail of hair from behind her neck and started to chew on it nervously. "You made a Sasquatch-Swear that you wouldn't tell anyone."

I nodded. "Don't give me a reason to break my promise."

Hannah spit out the rat tail and twirled the sloppy braid around her hairy finger. She smiled. "If you let me try them on, I'll let you taste the sweet sand and the delicious dirt."

"Why do you want to try the foot-hides so much?" I asked.

"They're different. They're fur-tastic," she answered.

Ever since I found out I had small feet, I had feared being different. I would have swapped hair with Hannah any day, because she was normal. And here she was trying to be different from everyone else. I had no idea why she'd want this curse.

"No way," I said. "The foot-hides are mine."

"The offer won't last long. Ruth is wolfing down the delicious dirt like it's water. In fact, she's started to mix it with water. Tastes great. Mmmm. You sure you don't want to try some?"

I shook my head.

"You're a bee sting in the butt," she said, huffing.

Ignoring her insult, I spun around and walked away. Suddenly, something crashed into the back of my legs. I tumbled to the ground, planting my face in a shrub. Hannah pulled at one of my foot-hides. I tried to kick her away, but she was too strong.

"Hairy armpits!" I yelled. "Get off."

"Let me wear them for a while. I want to know what they're like."

She sat on my butt and grabbed one of my legs, hauled it back and yanked at the foot-hide until it slipped off. She gasped.

"Sour berries! Your feet . . . they're so . . . they're so . . . tiny," she whispered. She rolled off me, dropping the foot-hide and scrambling backward, her eyes wide with amazement and her moustache curling up.

"I haven't fully bloomed yet," I explained.

"Hairballs," Hannah said. "That's why you're wearing the foot-hides. To hide your tiny tootsies. Wait until Ruth hears about this."

"You promised not to tell anyone," I said.

"About the foot-hides. Not about your feet," she said.

She got up and strode away, her rat tail of hair swishing from the back of her neck. The Hairyson sisters were great at spreading stories. I remembered that once they told a story about the Bone Eater. Every sasquatch in the tribe knew about the monster of the mountains that hunted sasquatchlings on full moon nights, but no one in our tribe had ever seen the beast. Hannah and Ruth whispered to a few sasquatchlings that they had seen the creature near the camp and by the end of the day, everyone was in a panic. I was sure every sasquatch would know about my feet by sunset.

I climbed a nearby fir tree and hid under the top branches, blending in with the spiky green needles, wishing I could hide from the tribe until my feet grew to the right size. I imagined the insults and laughter. I imagined Hannah and Ruth getting everyone to make up a song about my tiny pods. I imagined my beard curling into tight spirals while everyone pointed and laughed at me, while my parents hid in their cave home, ashamed.

High in the tree, I could see the valley below our mountain home. The forest covered the mountain like a yellowing meadow. A raven soared over the treetops and veered toward some white smoke coming from the base of the mountain. Was this the start of a forest fire? I had better head back home to warn the tribe.

At the very least, my news might distract the sasquatches from my tiny feet.

Grandma Bertha had a saying: "No time like now to pick the lice out of your hair." Sooner or later, I had to face the sasquatches, and I might as well do it now. I climbed down from the tree and headed back to the caves.

When I arrived, there was a great commotion. A group of sasquatches armed with branches and brush stood outside my parents' cave entrance. They were laying the foliage in front of the mouth of the cave.

Mom stomped toward the sasquatches with Yolanda Yeti close behind her. The white-haired sasquatch looked more like a sagging willow tree with all her years weighing her down. Still, she had the best hearing of all the sasquatches, probably because she had the biggest ears. Mom stuck her hairy fingers in her mouth and whistled. Everyone stopped working and gathered around her. I joined them, staying near the back. Were my tiny feet that much of a problem?

"First, let me put to rest the rumours running through the camp. The baldfaces have not declared war on us," she said.

The white smoke had to be from the baldface camp. The crowd murmured until Mom waved for silence. It took a few minutes for the chatter to die out.

"I've spoken to Yolanda Yeti about what she overheard when she was foraging at the base of the mountain," Mom said.

Yolanda Yeti cleared her throat and let out a harsh croak before she spoke. "The baldfaces are looking for us. I saw several of them with boom sticks. They were tracking some footprints near the base of the mountain. One of them talked about bringing back a sasquatch alive."

My hair curled. Had the baldfaces spotted Ruth and Hannah's tracks from our trip to the baldface camp earlier?

Everyone started talking at once. Mom waved her arms in the air. "Winter is near, which means the baldfaces won't be here for long."

Juniper Hairyson agreed. "Bernice Bigfoot is right. Remember thirty-seven summers ago, there were a bunch of baldfaces who tried to find us. They never did."

Some of the older sasquatches mumbled in agreement. The younger ones shook their heads and wondered aloud if these baldfaces were better hunters.

Mom waved her hand again. "Juniper is right. The baldfaces probably spotted some bear tracks or saw a grizzly and mistook it for one of us. They'll scour the mountain for a few days and find nothing. All we have to do is hide out until the first snowfall and then they'll be gone."

Dogger Dogwood, the sasquatch with the second biggest feet in the tribe, raised his hand. His sleek black hair was groomed so neatly, there wasn't even one mat or knot. He preened his eyebrow as he waited for the crowd to look his way. He was the tallest of the tribe, but you couldn't tell because he was always stooped over like he was ducking a low branch. He had lost the tribe leader vote to mom by a hair, and he never forgot about the loss.

"Bernice Bigfoot, if we hide now, we'll lose the opportunity to forage enough food for the winter. Would you have us starve?"

Dogger Dogwood made a good point, but in a bad way. He questioned Mom's leadership like a parent talking down to a sasquatchling. He constantly searched for some weak spot so he could knock her down in front of others, but Mom wasn't just the sasquatch with the biggest feet; she was also the wisest.

She said, "Dogger Dogwood might enjoy playing to your fears, but I like dealing with what I can smell, and I can smell baldfaces from thousands of strides away. Right now, I can barely pick up their scent. If they move further up the mountain, we have enough time to cover our caves, move beyond the valley and set up a temporary home. We can return here for our winter stores once the baldfaces are gone."

"Have you thought about what to do if they don't leave?" Dogger Dogwood asked, stroking his eyebrows.

"The baldfaces always leave the mountain for the winter."

"Waiting for them to leave? Is that really the best plan, Bernice Bigfoot? By the corn on my big toe, is that the best you can do?"

"We've survived many winters by staying hidden, Dogger Dogwood. Is your suggestion to fight the baldfaces?"

Sasquatches inched away from him. Others shook their heads and muttered to each other.

No one wanted to fight; not even Dogger Dogwood. He slouched lower and said nothing.

"Then it's settled. We will keep watch on the baldfaces. If they come closer, we will move. I'll lead a scout party to look for a temporary home in case we need it. Are there any volunteers?"

Grandma Bertha and Grandpa Benson raised their hands. They were the best sniffers in the tribe and were always up for an adventure. The tribe members twirled their moustaches and stroked their beards, signaling that they approved of Mom's solution. Only Dogger Dogwood and his family refused to touch their hairy faces. Instead, he grumbled and slunk off with his sister and two sons following.

"The rest of you, back to work," Mom ordered.

The sasquatches went back to covering the caves. Grandma Bertha and Grandpa Benson headed to the forest to gather berries for the long trip. Mom walked through the crowd, trying to calm everyone down, but when they asked how the baldfaces knew of our existence, the hair on her back stood straight up like porcupine quills. She growled that she had no answer, but swore she'd get to the bottom of it when she returned.

I didn't want to be around when she found out the truth.

Chapter Six

For two sunrises, the tribe worked to cover the caves with brush and wipe out the giant footprints along the trails. They moved wooden benches into the caves. They pulled apart the rocky fire pits and stomped the ashes into the dirt. Dad tried to keep everyone's spirits up by offering his special sasquatch chews. He dried out raspberries and turned them into little sticks of gummy treats. One taste of his sasquatch chew was enough to put a smile even on Dogger Dogwood's face. The sasquatches thanked Dad as he made his way through the tribe. While Mom and my grand-parents were gone, it was up to him to keep the tribe's spirits up.

I stayed out of everyone's way. I felt hair-ible about the work the tribe had to do, all because

I had shown myself to the baldfaces. No one except the Hairyson sisters knew I'd done it, but every time sasquatches glanced my way, I felt like they were accusing me with their arching eyebrows.

Ruth Hairyson stood a few strides away. Judging by the way she stared at my feet, Hannah must have told her everything. I ignored her, looking around for her sister. There was neither hide nor hair of her. I moved away from the crowd. Ruth started toward me. Before she could catch up, Hannah, out of breath, burst out of the woods. She grabbed her sister and pulled her aside. I followed the pair.

"Sour berries, the baldfaces are up to something," Hannah said, panting.

I straightened up. "What?"

Hannah gulped. "The baldfaces never did this before. It's new. It's different."

"What are they doing?" Ruth asked.

"They climbed some trees and placed weird things in the branches," she said.

"We should warn the tribe," I said.

"You do it. I want to see what the baldfaces did," Ruth said.

"I don't think this is a good idea," I warned, scratching my beard.

"Don't be a Scaredy-Squatch. If they're up to something, we need to be ready for it," Ruth said. "That's what Dogger Dogwood says."

The slouched-over sasquatch was turning many in the tribe to his way of thinking. I had to groom the Hairysons' hair and the best way to calm them down was to show them there was nothing to fear. I nodded for Hannah to show the way. She led us through the forest, down the mountain and through a gully. The yellow and orange leaves on the forest floor crunched under my heavy foot-hides, while the sisters moved with deer-like stealth. Ruth glanced back and glared as she shushed me. I tiptoed around the crunchy leaves, trying to keep quiet. I could just make out the faint odour of baldfaces. They had been here.

Hannah signaled for us to stop. She scanned the clearing while Ruth sniffed the air. I strained to hear any baldfaces, but all I heard was a brook and the chirping of a red-tailed chipmunk warning her family about us.

"Nothing's there," I said.

Ruth took a big whiff, her nostrils flaring wide enough to suck in the chirping chipmunk. "They're further down the mountain. Too far away to hear us."

Hannah pointed at the top of a tree. "There. There. See it?"

Ruth and I looked up. At the top of the bare tree was a giant black web. No spider could have created it. This had to be the work of the baldfaces.

Hannah took off for the tree before either Ruth or I could react. "Let's see what it does," Hannah whispered.

"It might be dangerous," I said.

She growled. "Everything is dangerous to you, Scaredy-Squatch. Who's with me?"

"I am," Ruth said.

The two sisters crept into the clearing toward the tall tree with the web across the branches.

"Wait for me," I said. I shuffled after them in my fake feet, wiping out their footprints with my own.

"WHOOP! WHOOP! WHOOP!" Suddenly, a deafening sound blared from all around us. A thousand honking geese couldn't have been louder than this racket. I covered my hairy ears and stepped back from the clearing. Ruth stopped in her tracks and yelled at her sister to come back, but Hannah reeled forward, clutching her ears, unable to hear her sister's warnings.

Suddenly a huge black web sprang up from the ground and carried Hannah up in the air. She screamed as the web closed around her. She screamed as she thrashed in the web. I stuffed my hair into my ears to block the hair-ible sound.

I ran to Ruth, who was doubled over with her hands over her ears, and pulled her back from the clearing and any other traps the baldfaces might have set.

"Get help!" I yelled.

"I have to save Hannah."

"The baldfaces are probably on their way right now," I said. "The racket must be a signal for them to come get us."

Ruth struggled as I pulled her away from her sister.

From inside the web, Hannah yelled, "Don't leave me!"

"Go," I ordered. "I'll get your sister."

"I'm not leaving," Ruth said. "Sasquatches stick together."

I was secretly glad for the help. "Okay. Fine. Then stick your hair in your ears and give me a hand," I instructed.

"What did you say?"

"Stuff your hair!" I yelled.

"You stuff it."

I motioned to her to stick her hair into ears like I had done. She finally understood and obeyed. Hannah squirmed in the giant web. I looked around for a way to tear down the web. I could hear Hannah's fearful shrieks. I could see Ruth's sweaty panic. But worst of all, I could smell the rotten lilac scent of the baldfaces getting closer.

"They're on their way," I said.

Ruth sniffed the air. "A lot of them."

Hannah screamed, "Hurry up!"

"Groom your hair!" I yelled. "We're going to get you down."

She couldn't hear me over the hair-ible noise.

"Ruth!" I yelled. "Try to find what this web is attached to."

Ruth nodded and started to look around the area. I scrambled away from the web, noticing something near the ground. A few strides from the web, a thin black vine was strung between two trees. I picked up a fallen branch and lobbed it at the vine. As soon as the wood hit the taut vine, another web sprang up from the ground, scattering leaves everywhere.

"Ruth, be careful," I said, jumping back. "There are more traps."

"I found something," she yelled back.

Ruth was pulling on a yellow vine wrapped around a tree. I started toward her, but I spotted a similar thick yellow vine wrapped around a nearby tree. I pulled on this vine. As I did, the web trap swung back and forth.

"Hurry up, Ruth!" Hannah yelled. "I can see them from here."

An acrid smell wafted up my nostrils. This smoky smell was not the kind from a fire but from something unnatural. The rolling caves. We had to move fast. I grabbed the vine and bit hard, cutting it in two. The web lowered a few feet, but Hannah still stayed up in the air.

"How close are they?" I shouted.

"They're maybe three hundred strides away," Hannah answered. "And moving fast!"

"Bite the vine," I yelled at Ruth.

"What?"

"Bite it!" I yelled again.

I nearly choked from the smell of smoke. The ground shook from the approaching baldfaces. Hannah howled inside the net. I had no choice.

"Ruth, free Hannah. Then head for home."

"What are you going to do?" Ruth yelled.

"I'm going to make sure the baldfaces don't come after you," I said as I sprinted away.

"Great mossy rock!" Ruth shouted. "Come back! Sasquatches stick together!"

I had made my decision. My foot-hides made a good amount of noise, which was just what I needed. I headed in the direction of the baldface smell. Two rolling caves hurtled toward me. A small black one led the way, followed by a large white one that shook the earth as it rumbled forward. These baldface machines kicked up loose leaves as they hurtled toward me.

I stood in the middle of the wide path until I was sure the creatures inside the rolling caves saw me. *Closer. Closer. Get closer.* The black cave was so close I could see the whites of the baldfaces' wide eyes. One of them pointed through the perma-ice window at me. Close enough.

I bolted into the woods, heading as far away from Ruth and Hannah as possible. The rolling caves came after me. I kept running up the slope. As I headed into a more heavily wooded area, I heard the machines stop. Had the baldfaces caught on? I stopped and peeked back. The rolling caves were too wide to go between the trees. The creatures shouted at each other while they grabbed long black boom sticks and jumped out. I turned and ran, leading the baldfaces deeper into the woods and away from the Hairyson sisters.

Branches slapped my body as I whizzed past the many trees. I ducked to avoid the heavier branches and picked up my feet to avoid the roots jutting out of the ground. I stumbled down a bank and crossed a shallow creek, soaking my foot-hides. Up the other side, I kicked up the fallen yellow leaves as I sprinted away from the shouts of baldfaces behind me. A few hundred strides into the woods, I found a shallow gully and hopped into it. I ran slowly along the gully to give the baldfaces a chance to catch up. I didn't want them to lose interest in me until I was sure the Hairysons had escaped. The baldfaces fell silent.

The gully grew deeper as I moved along it, but I crashed around, making enough noise to attract even the deafest of creatures. A fallen log blocked my way, forcing me to hop over it. THWOCK! A tiny arrow smacked into the wood just as I started to climb over. One of the baldfaces aimed a boom stick at me. I rolled over the log. THWOCK! Another little arrow hit the wood. I fell on my side, keeping my back to the log. The baldfaces were shooting at me, but these boom sticks didn't make any noise.

"Bigfoot's cornered. Get up high and cut off any escape routes," one of the baldfaces yelled.

How did they know my name? THWOCK! No time to wonder. I had to run. I caught my breath for a second. Then I crawled up the gully slope. Suddenly I felt a sting in my leg. A little arrow stuck in my thigh. I plucked it out.

"Ouch!"

Another arrow hit me in the back. I couldn't reach around to pull this one out. The baldfaces sounded closer. I clawed my way up the side of the gully. Handfuls of dirt and leaves came away in my hands until I reached the top. Then I sprinted for the woods.

The ground seemed uneven. I ran to one side, but when I tried to straighten up, the ground seemed to swell like waves on the lake. Everything around me started to spin. I smacked my face into a low-hanging branch. It should have hurt, but it tickled. I giggled. I tripped over a tree root and started to laugh really hard. My body felt as light as a duck feather, but my eyelids felt more like twin boulders. I snaked along the ground, laughing at how silly I must have looked.

"We've got it," a voice shouted.

"Catch me if you can," I tried to yell, but my tongue was thick as cold honey.

THWOCK! An arrow hit me in the butt. This one tickled like an ant crawling under my hair. No, more like a colony of ants crawling all over my hairy body. I tried to stand up, but my arms were like saplings and I was a clumsy cougar cub trying to climb up them. They gave way under my weight and I did a face plant into the loose soil. As I fell, I wondered if the Hairyson sisters got away. I hoped Hannah was safe. That was my last thought. Everything went black.

CHAPTER SEVEN

A dull pain in my right ear woke me up. I sat up in a dark cave, but it wasn't home. The surface under me felt weird: smooth like the lake when it froze over. I wished I had light to see where I was. The only light came from a blinking red star above my head. At first I thought I was looking at the night sky, but the red star didn't look right, just like the ground didn't feel right. I reached up to the lone light in the empty sky and my hand smacked into something hard.

"Ow!"

The smooth surface above me felt just like the surface under me and like the walls around me. I was inside some kind of cage. I was used to close spaces like my cave bedroom, but I could always smell where the fresh air was. Here, all I could smell was my fear.

"Hello?" I said. "Anyone here?"

No answer.

"Help! I'm in here."

Still no answer. I wished my mom was there. I wished my dad was there. I wished Grandma Bertha or Grandpa Benson were there. Hairy armpits! I'd even settle for Hannah or Ruth. I started to pound the wall.

"Let me out!"

The red light blinked at me.

"I want out!" I punched the wall. KER-RACK! Was that my hand breaking or the wall? I rubbed my knuckles. They were sore, but I could still bend my fingers. I punched again. CRACK! I was pretty sure the wall was breaking. This was my way out! I kept punching.

Suddenly my world shifted sideways. I tried to brace myself but I was sliding around the cave. My stomach flip-flopped as the cave rolled side to side. I felt like a robin chick in a nest that was blown out of the tree, except the chick could fly to safety. I could only crash into the wall.

Finally the world stopped shifting. I had to get out before everything started shifting again. I pounded at the wall with both hands. I was glad for the hairy pads on my knuckles, but my hands still stung from hitting the wall. It was like a thousand mosquitoes had landed under my hair and were biting me over and over again. I wound up and threw my right hand as hard as I could at the wall. Instead of stopping at the wall, my hand kept going through as bits of the wall rained on the ground. Fresh air blasted through the hole.

I pushed my face to the hole and sucked the cool air, then I backed up and attacked the wall again. Instead of punching, I kicked at it. My foot-hides protected my soles and I started to kick harder. The hole grew larger. More air rushed in. I felt the edges of the hole to check its size, then kicked again and again until the opening was large enough for me to crawl out.

The ground outside the cage felt rougher than the ground inside the little cave. I smelled something woody, but the scent was faint, overpowered by a bitter resin. I ran my hand along the surface. While I could feel the grooves of a wood grain, a slippery coating covered the surface.

The faint whistle of wind slipping through a crack perked up my ears. I crawled toward the sound. A slight breeze blew from somewhere in the large cave. I reached out in the dark. The breeze tickled the palm of my hands and the sweet smell of fresh air wiped away the sharp and bitter odour of the resin. Freedom was just a hair away.

"Marvelous."

I spun around, but it was too dark to see anything or anyone. I sniffed the air, but there was no scent of baldface; just the bitter resin on the ground.

"In my wildest dreams, I never would have even begun to imagine this moment. Tall as a cedar. Seven feet at least." The odd voice was coming from somewhere ahead of me. A square of light flicked on and the flash nearly blinded me. Blue-white light filled the space. The cage that had once held me was now visible. It was made of the same perma-ice I saw in the rolling caves. Bits of the ice from the wall I had kicked through littered the wooden floor, but the shards didn't melt.

Beyond the ice chamber, on the cave wall, the square of light beamed at me. Inside the square was a baldface. All I could see was his head, which had no hair anywhere, from the shiny top of his bald scalp to his bare chin. His ugly white smile made me uneasy, as if I were waiting for a cougar to attack.

"Easy, big fella. Very powerful creature. I'll have to double the strength of the next cage. Stay, big boy, stay. It's safer in the truck."

"Truck" must have been what the baldfaces called the rolling cave. I wondered how this creature could sneak up on me without giving off a scent.

He clapped his hands and smiled. "What a fine specimen you are."

"Are you going to eat me?" I asked.

The baldface's mouth dropped open. He gasped. "W-wh-what's this? You can talk!? Incredible. Say something else."

"Please don't hurt me."

He clapped his hands again, but the sound was weird, like he was far away, even though he looked like he was in the cave with me. As I moved closer, he watched me, but he was flat, like he was part of the wall.

"Amazing. How did you learn how to talk? Who taught you? Where did you learn?" he asked.

The story of tongues went far back in sasquatch history. Grandpa Benson told me a baldface came into our tribe, a baldface named Lysander. Well, he wasn't quite a baldface, because he was covered with hair. He wasn't as tall as a sasquatch, so he wasn't one of us either. Other baldfaces were hunting him. Feeling sorry for him, the tribe members took him in and protected him. In exchange, he taught us how to speak his language so we could spy on the baldfaces and protect ourselves from them. He claimed the baldfaces enjoyed hunting creatures that were different from them and warned the tribe to stay well away from these beasts. The tribe elders passed down his warning along with his gift of tongues.

I wasn't about to tell this baldface about the gift or anything else about the sasquatches. The less he knew about the tribe the better. "I don't taste good, and you'd get hair stuck in your teeth. Lots of it."

"I'm not going to eat you."

"Okay," I said. "Will you let me go?"

"This is so fantastic. What do they call you?" The baldface patted his chest. "Me, Dr. Samson." Then he pointed at me. "You? Your name?"

"Barnabas," I answered as I sidled to the side. Dr. Samson's green eyes tracked me as I moved around the truck. But when I moved to the side, I couldn't see the side of his face. I was always looking at the front of him.

"What do you want with me?" I asked.

"Why, I want your hair of course. Your beautiful shaggy hair."

I wrapped my arms around my chest. Suddenly I felt a thousand eyes looking at me the same way a screech owl eyes a family of wood rats. I tried to blend into the dim truck, but there was nowhere I could hide.

"Step in front of the camera. I want to get a better look," Dr. Samson said.

"The what?"

"The camera . . . The blinking red light."

The twinkling red light I'd seen earlier was high up on the cave wall. In the dim light of the square, I noticed the red light was attached to a black contraption with a single wide eye aimed at me.

"Step in front of the light. I can't see you too well where you're standing."

"Why don't you come here and look at me?" I said.

"Ah, yes, you have no idea about our technology. I'm not here. I'm actually in my university lab in Edmonton awaiting your arrival."

University? Technology? Edmonton? He was speaking gibberish. I had an easier time understanding the squawking crows that raided the tribe's vegetable garden.

"I don't know what you're saying," I said.

"It doesn't matter. All that matters is that I have Bigfoot."

How did he know my family name? Had he been spying on our tribe? "I'm not a Bigfoot," I lied.

"Your hair is going to make a lot of money." Dr. Samson cackled as he rubbed his hairless hands together.

"What is this moan-ee?" I asked.

The baldface stopped laughing and rolled up the sleeves of his white hide top.

"Money is the currency of my world. It's what funds my science experiments. It's what I'm about to get for this find of the millennium."

I shook my head, confused.

"I'm going to figure out what makes your hair grow so long and reduce it to a chemical formula. Bald men across the world will do anything for my formula for hair growth. I'll call it Sasquatch Shampoo."

"You want to look like a sasquatch?" I asked.

"No, I want the hair that used to be up here." He patted his bare head. "You're going to help me get it back."

"There's no such thing as a sasquatch," I lied.

"I'll know for sure when you arrive in Edmonton." He picked up a shimmering cross and snipped it open and shut a couple of times like a bird's beak snapping at a worm. I did not like the look of these snip-snaps. I had to think fast. I had to make him think he had the wrong sasquatch. For once I was glad for my feet.

"Does this look like a Bigfoot?" I asked. I ripped the hair off my fake feet and lifted up a leg.

The baldface squinted for a second, then his eyes suddenly popped open wide. "What the — let me see your feet."

"Ha, ha!" I said. "You fell for my trick!"

The red-cheeked baldface put his hand to his ear and yelled, "Get someone into the back of the truck. I need you to get a look at the creature's feet!"

Suddenly, the cave lurched forward and I slid into the ice cage. The shattered pieces on the ground slid toward the baldface. Dr. Samson shouted at me, but he didn't make any sense.

"Get in the truck. Hurry up. I need to see his feet."

"Are you talking to me?" I asked.

He ignored me, but it didn't matter. The cave stopped moving. Now all I had to do was widen the crack at the back. I knelt down and followed the whiff of fresh air, but as I neared the wall I heard footsteps and voices outside. The smell of rotten lilacs filled my nose. The baldfaces were near.

"Open the door!" yelled Dr. Samson.

The wall lifted straight up, blinding me with light. Cold air blasted inside the room, along with a flurry of snow.

"He's out of the cage!" yelled one of the baldfaces.

"I got him," the other one said as he lifted his boom stick at me. He had a big nose and a strange black patch over one eye.

"Don't shoot," yelled Dr. Samson. "I need him alive."

The baldface with the patch over his eye ordered the others, "Stand down. Okay, big fella, you're safe. Nothing to worry about." He scratched under his eye patch and smiled, then reached behind his back.

I roared and jumped over him. The others froze, their mouths gaping open. I hopped over them and landed in a snowdrift. Then I ran as fast as I could. The blizzard was nearly blinding. Between the snow and the dark night I could barely see ten strides in front of me, but that meant the baldfaces couldn't see either. I ran ahead as fast as I could, letting the blowing snow wipe out my trail. Behind me, the baldfaces screamed after me. I ran until their voices faded in the blizzard. I was safe from them, but now I had a bigger problem. Where in the hairy tangle was I?

Chapter Eight

The winter air here smelled different. No mountains. No pine trees. No sasquatches. Instead, baldface garbage, baldface smoke, baldface sweat. Grandma Bertha used a word to describe this stench. She called it pull-ution. She had smelled it when she was a scout sent to keep an eye on the baldfaces. She described how it attacked her nose and made her throat burn, just as the air was doing to me now. Pull-ution sounded exactly like the right word to describe the smell, because it made me want to pull my burning throat out.

The wind whipped around me, tossing bits of snow against my fur like white brambles. My thick hair protected me from the cold, but the blizzard was getting worse. I had to find shelter and fast. I walked through the blinding snowstorm, hoping to pick up the scent of my woods. I slipped every few strides because of my foot-hides. I lost track of the number of strides I had walked. The blowing snow stuck to my fur, turning me as white as Yolanda Yeti. As I trudged through the snow, the smell of the baldface world grew stronger. No matter which way I turned, I smelled rotting lilacs and smoke. I couldn't turn back because Dr. Samson's tribe members were behind me. All I could do was stumble forward.

Every now and then I could see yellow globes of light over me. Sometimes, I spotted a light that flashed red, green and yellow. The snow let up once to give me a glimpse of rows of baldface shelters on either side. I moved on, hoping no one could see me. I travelled for what seemed like forever until I lost all sense of direction.

Wham! I ran into something hard and flat. It was a perma-ice wall with strange black symbols across it. The symbols reminded me of the cave drawings at home, except these weren't pictures. They looked more like a strange collection of tiny twigs laid out in rows.

On the other side of the wall, there was no snow. The ground was as white as snow, but it had a weird sheen, like the resin in the truck. Lining either end of this wide clearing were smaller cave entrances with perma-ice walls. Inside were baldface goods. One cave was filled with foot-hides. Another one had top-hides. One had hides for legs. Even though this was the inside of a large cave, there was enough light to see. It was like the baldfaces had moved the sun into their cave.

At the far end of the clearing, a group of baldfaces carried flat boards attached to sticks. The white boards were marked with twiggy symbols.

Even though this cave looked warm, there were too many baldfaces inside. I wondered if I could blend into this world. It was much easier in the forest where there were trees and bushes. This cave didn't offer many places to hide. If these baldfaces with the white boards were part of Dr. Samson's tribe, I'd be in big trouble, but the blizzard wasn't going to let up any time soon and I started to feel the cold through my snow-covered hair.

Before I could do anything, a black furry hand grabbed my arm. The hand felt smooth and soft and belonged to a creature that was bundled up in a bright red hide that covered most of its body, arms and head. A strange blue hide wrapped around the beast's face, like a layer of fur. I could only see the creature's eyes.

A muffled voice asked, "Are you going into the mall or not?"

Mall? That must be what the baldfaces called this giant cave.

"You stay out here and you'll freeze to death," the baldface said.

The creature reached past me, grabbed an outcropping of the perma-ice wall and pulled. The wall swung open, letting warm air blast out. I took one look at the blowing snow, then at the warm cave . . . and I stepped inside.

Past the perma-ice wall, I shuffled to one of the cave walls, while I watched the baldface stamp the snow off its black foot-hides, which had little tufts of grey fur sticking out. I wondered if this was its natural hair or the fur of a hunted animal. The baldface pulled off the black-hides that covered its hairless hands and slapped them against the blue hides that covered its legs. The snow fell to the shiny ground and melted into tiny pools of brown water. The beast then unraveled the blue hide over its face and pulled back the red hide from its head to reveal a green-eyed, pale face with orange hair only on the top of its head. It was a baldface girl.

Her bright orange hair looked like the sky at sunset. She ignored me as she brushed the snow off her face-hide. Then she opened the inside perma-ice wall and walked into the large cavern. She glanced back, holding the wall open for me. I followed her into the giant cave.

A baldface halfway down the cave noticed me. She wore bright hides and carried a stick with a board attached to the top. She yelled, "There's one of the animal killers!"

The others turned and spotted me. A few waved their white boards in anger. Several pointed at me. A couple started to run forward with white stones in their hands.

One female baldface screeched, "Fur is murder!"

Another one yelled, "Fur is forbidden!"

A skinny male baldface with spiky blond hair stepped forward, holding up a thin white stone. He cried out, "Make an example out of the animal killer." The porcupine-headed baldface shook the stone, making a rattling sound. “Paint him blood red!!”

They all ran toward me. Their faces reminded me of cougars about to pounce. I backed up and pushed open the perma-ice walls and slipped into the blizzard. I jumped into the snow and rolled around, gathering all the snow on to my fur. Then I sprang up and ran along the side of the giant cave wall, hoping I had enough snow on my fur to blend in.

The baldfaces burst, yelling and screaming, out of the mall. A sickly sweet smell made me wince. The odour was enough to make me dizzy, and it was coming from the rattling white stones the baldfaces were carrying. I stopped and pressed myself against the snow-covered wall.

They looked left and right, but they didn’t see me. Porcupine Head started to walk in my direction. I slammed against the smooth wall, hoping he hadn’t seen me. His blue hide clung to his body as the wind picked up. He moved closer. A few more strides and he’d spot me.

“There he is,” yelled the young baldface girl with the bright orange hair.

Porcupine Head turned around and ran away while the young baldface motioned the others to hurry up. She watched them run away and then looked right at me.

"Hurry up. They'll be back soon," she said.

I didn't move.

"I can see you," she said.

Hairy armpits, this baldface had sharp eyes. I wasn't sure if I could trust the orange-haired creature, but I knew that if I stayed outside, either Dr. Samson or the angry baldfaces would find me. I stepped away from the wall and walked toward her.

"Thank you."

"I'm Jamie," she said, holding out her hairless hand.

At first, I thought she wanted to attack, but she left her hand up in the air. I leaned down and sniffed her hand, which smelled like sweet cherries. She pulled her hand away.

"Are you nuts?" she asked.

Nuts? Why would she think I was a nut? I didn't think I looked like a hazelnut. I shook my head, confused.

"Sorry," I mumbled. "I am Barnabas."

"You should be sorry. Just because you see a sasquatch sighting on the news, you think it's funny to run around in a sasquatch costume and get everyone worked up. Did you know the Citizens for Animal Protection were going to be here to protest against the fur shop that just opened up? Yeah, I suppose you did if you came in that get up. Pee-yew, it stinks."

I shook my head. I had no idea what she'd just said.

"They've been on the radio and TV all week long."

I shrugged, hopelessly confused.

"Let's find you a safe place," she said, "before the CAP-pies come back."

"Thank you for helping me," I said.

"Yeah, yeah, yeah. I have a soft spot for class clowns who get in over their heads. Get inside."

I stomped my foot-hides on the ground just as Jamie had done earlier. The more I could imitate a baldface, the better chance I had of fitting in. She led me through the clearing. A couple of baldfaces in the caves gaped at me as I walked past. I walked a little faster. Jamie had to jog to keep up.

"What a dumb stunt," Jamie said. "You might look like the sasquatch on TV, but that's not going to get you on the news."

The best thing to do when I didn't know what the baldface was talking about was to apologize. Jamie stopped scolding me. We walked through the giant cavern in silence.

When we reached the area where the angry baldfaces had been, I was stunned to see exactly how large this cavern was. Wide paths split into three more directions with dozens of caves along each path. Above, there was another level of caves. I felt like I was in the middle of a baldface mountain.

"We have to get to the second floor," Jamie said. "This way."

She led me down a path. On either side, the caves were filled with strange shiny trinkets and more strange bright symbols on the perma-ice walls. Down the middle of the path was a row of trees. Even though it was winter, these trees had leaves. Their scent reminded me of home. Halfway down the path were grey and black steps that moved on their own to the top level. The baldfaces must have had very weak legs if they couldn't climb the steps by themselves.

"Hey!" a voice cried out. "Stop right there."

I turned and saw a male baldface pointing at me. He didn't look pleased. Jamie froze. I looked around for a place to hide but saw nothing. I was trapped!

CHAPTER NINE

The baldface in dark blue hides lumbered toward us. He was short and skinny, but he seemed to lumber as if he were a grizzly bear on hind legs. Jamie grabbed my hand and pulled me closer.

"What is he doing in this mall with that costume?" the baldface asked.

"It's okay, Alvin. He's with me. It's a promotional stunt."

"No one cleared it through me. You know anything in the mall has to get the green light from yours truly." He eyed me up and down. I said nothing, my back hair starting to stand on end.

"Sorry, Alvin. I'm sure my mom forgot. I'll get her to send you the forms."

"In triplicate. What's the stunt anyway, Jamie?"

"You'll go ape over our coffee," she said.

The male baldface named Alvin laughed. "Not bad."

My hair lowered and I even managed to crack a smile as I pretended to understand what they were talking about. "Sorry," I said.

"Sorry for what," Alvin asked.

"Uh . . . um . . . well." I looked to Jamie.

She shook her head. "He can't hear too well with the head on. Listen, Alvin, I don't want to freak you out, but I think the protestors are vandalizing the mall," she said.

Alvin stared at my face. "What makes you so sure, Jamie?"

"They have cans of spray paint."

He turned away. "Really? This is excellent. I missed my karate class last night and I need a work out."

"You'd better hurry," Jamie said. "I saw them outside."

Alvin pulled out a thin black box attached to his hides with a curly black vine and spoke into it.

"Code blue. I repeat. Cold blue," he barked.

The talking box answered back: "Roger!"

He ran away from us, still holding the talking box.

"I thought his name was Alvin," I said. "Who's Roger?"

"Har, har. Come on, my mom's cafe is over here," Jamie said, pulling me along. "But we'd better go in the back way. You're attracting way too much attention dressed the way you are. Head to the door."

She led me to a wall and pushed open a section of it — the door — and led me along a narrow path lit by glowing tiles on the wall above. The white walls were smooth and beige and the pathway was completely straight and even, unlike any cave or trail I had ever seen. Under the light, my fur looked dull and dirty, while Jamie's face almost looked green.

We headed down the path until Jamie stopped at a black section of the wall.

"What's this?" I asked.

"The door to the back of my mom's coffee shop."

I didn't know what coffee meant, but now I was sure what door meant. It was a covered entrance.

Jamie plucked a silver leaf from her bag and jammed the pointed end into a silver circle in the door. She turned the leaf and the circle clicked. She reached down, grabbed a round knob and opened the door. The smell of delicious dirt wafted from inside the chamber.

The familiar smell made me think of Hannah and Ruth. Jamie pushed me through the entrance, but I bonked my head on the top of the opening. I ducked low and moved inside. Behind me, Jamie closed the black door. The scent of delicious dirt came from several brown boxes sitting in the cramped white-walled cave. The stink of baldfaces was near. Jamie grabbed my back hair and pulled.

"First thing we have to do is get rid of your costume," she ordered as she pulled harder.

"Ow," I said. "Careful! It's my hair."

She pulled again. I yelped. She stopped.

"Whoa, this *is* your hair," she said, wide-eyed with wonder. "What did you do? Did you use super glue?"

"What's super glue?" I asked.

"You know, glue that's super."

I shrugged. "I don't know."

She scanned up and down my body, her bright green eyes staring intently at every strand of hair. She stopped when she saw my hairy face. She reached up to touch it. I jumped back and hit my head on the top of the cave. Jamie stared at me in the same way that Dr. Samson ogled me. Her wide eyes and slack jaw was the same look I had seen Grandma Bertha give me when she first saw my tiny feet — disbelief.

"Why did you help me get away from the baldfaces?" I asked, trying to distract her.

"The what?" She wouldn't stop gawking at me.

"The baldfaces. The ones who wanted to get me."

"You're not from around here, are you?"

I shook my head.

"Well, Barnabas, I helped because you looked like you couldn't help yourself," she said. "I've been picked on enough to know how it feels, but I stand up for myself. My mom says it's the Irish in me. It looked like the protestors weren't going to stop long enough to hear you explain that you were just pulling a dumb prank. I couldn't walk away, even if you got yourself in this mess."

I had no idea what she meant, so I went back to the safe thing to do when in doubt. "Sorry."

She shrugged. "No biggie." For the first time, I noticed little brown dots all over her face. If her cheeks were the night sky, these dots were the stars. I leaned closer to get a better look.

"Hey!" she yelled, "get out of my face."

I jumped back and hit my head again on the top of the cave. Dust rained down on both of us.

"Sorry," I said. "I've never seen dots like that before."

"They're called freckles."

"They're really nice."

"People always bug me about them. I wish they were gone."

I shook my head. "Why?"

"I hate them."

"Why?"

"I just do."

"There has to be a reason."

"Anyone ever tell you that you're too nosy?"

"No. Do the freckles hurt your face? Is that why you want to get rid of them?" I couldn't look away at the bare skin on the girl's face and the fur-tastic dots.

"It's because they make me look like a freak, okay?"

"Sorry."

"And stop apologizing for everything," she ordered. "It's irritating."

"Sorry."

She glared at me and said nothing more. Even though she was a baldface she was like me. She had trouble fitting in, except her problem was her freckled face, while mine was my feet. I wondered if we had any other things in common.

"Well, I like them," I said.

"Barnabas, you must be sweating under that costume. Take it off."

"I can't," I said.

"If you don't take it off, the fur protestors are going to find you and give you a paint bath."

"I mean I can't take it off."

"The joke's over. Stop pretending to be a sasquatch," she said. "Take off the mask." She moved toward me and reached for my beard.

"No. Don't. Please."

"Why not?"

"Because."

"Is it because you're naked under the costume? I promise I won't look."

Should I tell this baldface the truth? Could I trust her? She had trusted me with the truth about her freckles, and I needed an ally in this baldface world. I took a deep breath and told my secret: "I am a sasquatch."

Jamie laughed. "Are you insane? You're just a geek with too much time on his hands."

"It's the hairy truth," I said.

She shook her head. "You're a super hairy class clown."

There had to be some way to get her to believe me.

"Pull my hair," I said, thrusting my face toward her.

"I know this joke. It's a lame version of pull my finger," she said.

"Please, pull my hair," I said.

"Whatever." She reached up, grabbed my chin hair and yanked. Ow. Did it ever hurt!

"Did you glue this on too?" she grunted.

"Hairy armpits!"

She yanked a few hairs out and examined my face.

"Oh my goodness, it's real hair," she said. "I mean it's really growing out of you."

I rubbed my sore chin and nodded. "And it's the same all over."

"What are you?" she asked. The wild look in her eyes looked all too familiar. It was the same look I saw in a marten's eyes when it sniffed a nearby wolf. She was scared. What surprised me was the fact that she didn't run.

"Tell me what you are," she demanded.

"I'm a sasquatch."

"No, what are you really?"

"It's true, Jamie. You have to believe me."

She leaned forward, still checking out my hairy body. "Where are you from?"

"The mountains, but some baldfaces were hunting our kind."

Jamie narrowed her eyes. "Why?"

I told her my story, describing Dr. Samson, the hairless creature who didn't even have eyebrows, and how he wanted to use me to cure baldness. I told her about my escape from the truck and how I needed to get back home.

"So you think a completely bald man and a guy with an eye patch are after you?"

I nodded.

"For your hair."

"Right."

She rolled her eyes. I hoped that was a good sign.

"He said he wanted to do tests on me," I said.

"Oh, I get it. So is this Dr. Samson a psychiatrist?"

"What? I don't know."

"It all makes sense." She cocked her head to the side and clucked at me the same way that Mom clucked at young sasquatches when they stood on their toes to see who was taller. "Where did you say your home was?"

"The mountains."

"Which ones?"

"We call them the mountains."

"I think I might be able to find out, but it may take some time. You'll have to stay here for a while."

I beamed. "Does that mean you'll help me?"

Jamie nodded. "I'm a sucker for stray puppies, and you're about as stray as they come."

I wrapped my hairy arms around Jamie in a bear hug. She squirmed in my grip.

"How long do you think you were with Dr. Samson?"

"I don't know. They shot me with a little arrow that made me sleep."

She stiffened. "Why did they do that?"

"I told you. Dr. Samson wanted to take my hair. He's bad."

She started to back up. "Take it easy, Barnabas. No need to get upset."

"Please don't leave."

"Relax. You need some professional help." She headed to the door.

I shook my head. "I think I should go."

"Where to?"

"Anywhere where there are no baldfaces."

Jamie stopped moving and chewed her bottom lip. "I don't think that will be very good for you."

"I have to go," I said.

"Maybe this Dr. Samson can help you get better," she suggested.

My eyes welled up. "Please don't send me back to him. He scares me."

Jamie hesitated, looking me up and down. Finally, she spoke. "Don't worry. I won't.

Promise. At the very least, we should let your parents know you're okay."

"You'll help me?"

She smiled. "Like I said, I'm a sucker for strays."

"Thank you, thank you."

"Just don't have another meltdown on me."

"How are you going to find them?"

"I guess I have to look for where *sasquatches* hang out," she said, rolling her eyes. I wasn't sure what her look meant.

"If you get me close enough to the mountains, I'll find my way home," I said.

"Okay, I'll keep that in mind," she said. "I mean, that's a good idea."

I smiled.

"You'll have to hide out in the mall for a while," she said.

"How long?"

"I don't know. It could take some time. What's your last name, Barnabas?"

"Bigfoot."

Jamie scrunched her face at me. "Of course it is."

"We have to go now, before Dr. Samson shows up."

"Relax, Barnabas. You're not going anywhere yet. We need to get you cleaned up," Jamie said.

"What do you mean?"

"You stink. When was the last time you had a bath?"

I sniffed my armpits, but they didn't smell bad. I smelled exactly the same as any other sasquatch. Then the truth dawned on me. I smelled like a sasquatch. I didn't smell like a baldface, and I certainly didn't look like one either. There was no way I could blend in with these creatures. Not unless...

"I have to be more like your kind," I said.

Jamie cocked her head to one side, her orange hair cascading like a little waterfall. "Okay, that's a good start. What were you thinking?"

"We have to get rid of my hair."

CHAPTER TEN

The problem was how to get rid of my hair. It would take too long and hurt too much to rip out every strand, but Jamie had a plan.

"I'm going to shave your face and get you some clothes."

"What are clothes?" I asked.

"These." She pointed at her own bright-coloured hides.

"I don't think they'll fit me."

"Silly. I meant I'll find you some clothes. Wait here and don't leave. Not for anything. Understand?"

I nodded. She left. Alone, I had a chance to sniff around the room. Square brown containers reeked of delicious dirt. On a wooden shelf sat leaf-thin white circles. Maybe these were hides for the top of a baldface head. Beneath the shelf was a collection of round perma-ice containers with single ears on the sides. They reminded me of the hollowed-out wooden cups we used to drink water, but they were much smaller. Behind the perma-ice cups were straight pink twigs. The smell of delicious dirt beckoned me, and I pulled open the flap of one of the brown containers and peeked inside at golden coloured bags that looked identical to the one the Hairyson sisters had found at the baldface camp. I pulled one out.

What could it hurt to try the dirt? I poked a hole in the bag. Sure enough, the ground dirt tumbled out. I dipped a finger into the bag, scooped up a bit of the bitter grounds and sucked on my finger. The bitter taste danced across my tongue like a dozen ants looking for their anthill. Not bad. But where was the sweet sand?

I scoured the shelves, sniffing everything and wincing from the assault of baldface odours. Finally, I found a thin white and blue flat container at the bottom of the shelf. A faint smell like honey wafted from inside. Eagerly, I broke open the container, which peeled away easily, only to find strange white cubes inside.

I plucked a cube out and placed it on my tongue. Sweet and yummy, like sweet sand. I tried another cube. Then another. And then I poured some delicious dirt into my mouth. Then another sweet sand cube. Before I knew it, I had eaten the contents of the container and all the delicious dirt in the golden bag.

I slid the empty bag and container to the back of the light brown shelf, feeling guilty for eating Jamie's food without asking her, but I convinced myself she wouldn't mind. Besides, I was starving.

Suddenly, I heard a strange buzzing, almost like a bee had zipped through my head and was looking for the queen in a hive. I shook my head to shake out the bee, but the buzzing grew worse. My legs began to twitch. I forced myself to sit on the ground while I placed my hands on my legs to settle them down. The hair on my arms looked like they were vibrating. Or was it my eyes that were vibrating?

The cave walls seemed to close in on me and the air turned stale. I needed fresh air *right now.* I staggered to my feet and searched for a way out. Which one of the two doors did I come through? I stumbled to the one on the left and opened it. Through the door was a baldface nightmare. Baldfaces seated at tables pointed and screamed as I stumbled ahead.

A female baldface with the same orange hair as Jamie grabbed a white branch with black bristles and swatted me. I raised my arms to protect myself, but she pushed the black bristles against my body and forced me backwards. The smell of delicious dirt filled my nostrils. The strange smells and the squawking baldfaces were too much for me to handle. I let out a sasquatch growl, but it came out more like a burp, followed by liquid hairballs.

The female backed away. When I stopped spewing up liquid hairballs, she charged at me with her white branch. I bolted out of the cave and into the large cavern. I didn't know which way to turn, but I knew I had to run away from the crazy baldface trying to hit me.

I staggered from one cave entrance to another, looking for a way out, but the more I stumbled, the dizzier I got. I stumbled into the baldface Jamie had talked to earlier, the one with the blue hides and the talking box. What was his name again? Alvin. He reeked of cougar sweat.

"Oh no you don't. Not until I get the forms in triplicate," said Alvin. I spotted a shiny silver pin on his chest.

"Ooh, shiny," I said.

"Don't touch. You're in enough trouble already. I know you stirred up the protestors with your fur stunt, kid. You're going home."

"Hairy armpits! Thank you, thank you, thank you," I said as I tried to hug Alvin. My tongue started to feel heavy.

"Buddy, you reek," the baldface said as he grabbed me by the arm and dragged me forward.

"I want to go home," I said.

"Enough games, kid. You're out of here. Don't make me go kung fu on your butt." His tiny hand had a firm grip on my arm, which now felt like a wilting daffodil. I skidded along the ground, trying to pull away from him, but I was too weak.

Then Jamie ran up to us. "It's okay, Alvin, it's okay. I'm here," she yelled. She carried baldface hides in her arms.

"What's wrong with this guy?"

"His costume's too hot. He's got some heat stroke. I have to get him some water before he gets delirious." she explained.

Alvin crossed his arms. "I don't like the looks of him. He's going to scare customers off."

Jamie grabbed my hand and squeezed it tight. "Don't worry, Alvin. I'll make sure he doesn't cause any trouble. Once I get him out of this costume and give him some air, he'll be fine."

"Okay, Jamie. I'll let him go this time, but if I see him one more time in that outfit, I'm calling the cops on him for making a public disturbance. That's a 4-15, you know."

Jamie nodded and led me away. She led me down the narrow path again and pushed me into the cramped cave.

"What's wrong with you?" she said. "I told you to stay put. And why do you smell like coffee?"

I pointed at one of the golden bags of delicious dirt. "Yum," I mumbled.

"How much coffee did you eat?" Jamie asked.

"That's what you call it? Pretty name," I said.

"What happened, Barnabas, after you ate the coffee?"

"I went out that door and ran into a baldface with orange hair who tried to hit me. She was very, very, very angry."

"You ran into my mom? Oh man, she's probably freaking out. Here, put these clothes on." She threw the baldface hides in my lap. "This time, don't leave. I mean it." Then she headed through the door.

I picked up a blue hide that looked like a pair of legs and a red and black hide that seemed more like something to go over my body. I tried to shove my legs through the holes in the hide, but my baldface foot-hides were too large. I had to kick them off to put on the hides. As I tried to put these things on, I also practiced the word Jamie used for the hides: "Cuh-lows. Cuh-lows. Clothes."

The clothes felt snug against my body. My hair was crushed under the itchy blue hides, which hugged my thighs, but left my shins uncovered. The red hide left much of my hairy forearms uncovered as well as much of my chest, but it wasn't as snug as the blue hides. I tried to put my fake feet back on.

Jamie rushed back into the cave and closed the door behind her. She scowled at me. "You puked in the coffee shop. Mom's furious."

"Sorry. She hit me with a big white branch."

"Big white what . . . oh, her broom. Yeah, well, just remember the broom the next time you get the bright idea to go for a walk in the mall."

"I won't do that again," I said.

"Whoa! Hold on there, Barnabas. What are those?" Jamie pointed at the fake foot in my hand.

"I'm a late bloomer. My feet haven't grown to full size yet. I wear these foot-hides to hide the fact." I waited for the teasing to begin.

"Foot-hides? You're really playing up this sasquatch thing. Okay, they're not foot-hides. They're shoes."

"Shoo."

"Shoes."

"Shoes."

"Yes. Now take the fake hair off the shoes and you'll fit right in."

Hairy armpits, my small feet actually helped me in the baldface world. I pulled the hair off so that only the whites of the shoes were visible.

"Pee-yew, you really need some deodorant," Jamie said. "You smell like over-ripe bananas."

She handed me a grey tube and motioned me to rub it under my armpits. I did as she asked.

"No, take the cap off first," she said. She reached over and plucked the cap from the tube and motioned me to rub the tube against my armpits.

"What's this for?" I asked. The smell of rotten lilacs greeted my nose. This was the smell of baldfaces.

"They'll cover up your smell."

"This reeks," I said.

"Not as bad as you do. Now finish getting dressed."

I squirmed in the clothes Jamie had gathered for me. Snug against my body, the clothes flattened out my hair like long grass under a boulder. I wanted to scratch every inch of my covered body.

"These clothes don't cover me," I said.

"Button up your shirt." She pointed at the red hide.

"I thought you called the hides clothes," I said.

She sighed. "Yes, they are clothes, but more specifically, the top is a shirt and the bottoms are jeans."

"Oh," I said.

She pulled the red shirt closed over my chest and threaded little white circles through holes in the hide. Then she fastened the little circle at the waist of the blue hide.

"The shirt and jeans will cover most of your body hair," she said.

"Not all," I said, pointing down at my hairy shins.

She groaned. "Okay, here. Try these on." She reached into a bag and pulled out two long white snake skins. "They're socks. Put them over your feet."

I took them and tried to fit one of the snake skins over my shoe, but she stopped me.

"Under the shoes," she said, pulling off my shoes and helping me into the snake skins. She yanked them up high on my legs so all my leg hair was covered by either the jeans or the socks. I walked around, looking at the strange clothes.

"I look like a baldface," I said.

"Not quite. This will take care of the rest." She pulled out a thick black rock with a silver top. She pushed a button and the rock started to buzz like angry bees were caught inside.

I froze. "What is that?"

"Don't be scared. It's a shaver," Jamie said. "This won't hurt."

She pushed the box of bees toward my face, but I flinched.

"What does it do?"

"It'll take your hair off. Relax."

I looked at the buzzing shaver, then at Jamie. Either I could trust her or I couldn't. I nodded, then I shut my eyes. The buzzing grew louder. The shaver brushed against my hair. At first, it tickled. Then, the shaver yanked my hair off my chin.

"Ow!" I yelped. "That hurts."

"Sorry, but your hair is so long, it's catching. I'll try to be more careful."

My back hair stiffened as she approached with the shaver, but I braced myself for the attack. I could hear the shaver rasp against my hair, sometimes plucking out a hair. I gritted my teeth against the pain as she moved the buzzing box across my cheeks, chin and forehead.

Soon, the hair pulling stopped, replaced by the strange vibrating feeling of something cold across my bare skin. I shuddered.

She clicked off the shaver and stood back. "Not bad. Not bad at all."

"Are you done?"

She shook her head. "Now the hands."

I stuffed my hands under my armpits. "Do you have to?"

"I couldn't find gloves big enough for you. Hold out your hand."

I drew one hand from under my armpit and held it out. She turned on the shaver and ran it against the back of my hand. I felt a thousand stings. "Hairy armpits!"

"You want me to shave your armpits?" she asked.

"No, no, I'm fine."

She shrugged. "Not bad, if I do say so myself."

"I think I've had enough." I tried to pull my hand back, but she had a firm grip around my wrist.

"Almost done," she said. "Just be patient."

I watched the shaver mow down my hand hair, stunned to see the pale white flesh underneath. At my feet, a pile of my hair grew larger with each pass of the shaver. I was losing myself, one hair at a time.

Finally she turned off the shaver.

"Okay, that wasn't so bad, was it?"

I stared at the pile of what used to be me on the ground.

"Now the other hand."

I gritted my teeth and held out the other hand. This time the shaver hurt less, but it was probably because I was more interested in my bare hand. The pale flesh looked like a barren field of snow, with only an odd tree poking out. This didn't look like my hand any more.

Jamie clicked off the shaver. "Okay, done. Do you want to see my handiwork?"

I looked at both hands now, stunned at how naked I seemed. She reached behind her and grabbed a little circle of perma-ice. She put it in front of me.

"It's a mirror," she said. "So you can see yourself."

I looked into the mirror, but I didn't see myself. I saw a baldface looking back at me. He scrunched his broad nose and squinted his brown eyes. It was a hideous creature with the palest skin I had ever seen. Even whiter than

Yolanda Yeti's hair. I bared my teeth at him. He bared his yellow teeth right back at me.

"That's you," Jamie said. "Without hair."

"I'm ugly," I said. "I'm so bald."

"Only where you're supposed to be," she said.

I looked back at the reflection of myself. Once I got used to looking at the baldface version of me, I couldn't stop staring at myself. I had never seen my bare skin before. I rubbed my chin, which felt smooth like a rock polished in the river. The brown hair on my head was still there, but it looked like a horse's mane.

Jamie said, "You'll fit right in."

I looked at myself in the mirror again. Would I ever look normal again? Would my hair grow back? Would anyone in my tribe even recognize me? I'd never felt more alone than I did right now.

Jamie patted my smooth hand and smiled. "You'll get used to it," she said.

I said nothing.

She added, "And it'll grow back in no time."

"I look so different," I said.

"No, you look like us," she said. "And you're kind of cute."

If I'd had any cheek hairs, they'd have been curling right about then.

"I'm joking," Jamie said. "But you do look better without the facial hair."

"Easy for you to say," I said. "You don't have any."

"And I'd like to keep it that way. My aunt has a moustache. Not a good look."

"You might look good with a moustache," I suggested.

Jamie glared at me.

"A goatee would make you look beautiful."

"Shut up." She slapped my arm.

"How about huge sideburns?" I said. "You'd make a cool-looking sasquatch with all orange hair."

"Keep it up and I'll shave the rest of you," Jamie said.

"Please don't," I said.

She laughed. She touched my bare hand. Her smooth skin felt warm against me. I smiled and put my other hand on top of hers. Together, we scooped up the hair and threw it into a short white container near the door. When we were done, the container was overflowing with hair.

I rubbed my face with my bare hands. This was going to take some getting used to.

"Jamie, what do we do now?" I asked.

"We find out where you're from. I checked the internet. There's no report of runaway kids in Alberta."

"I didn't run away. Dr. Samson took me."

"Oh right, because you're a sasquatch. Wait a minute, there was a news report about a sasquatch sighting in B.C. Is that where you got this idea?"

"Take me to this B.C.," I said.

"I can't do that."

"Why not?"

"We have to be sure that's where you're from first. I'll show you some pictures of the B.C. mountains."

"But you said you couldn't take me there."

"I'll show you pictures, like the one on the wall." She waved at an etching on the wall: Jamie with the orange-haired baldface who attacked me earlier.

"Oh, an etching," I said.

She sighed. "Yeah, sure. Do you want to see my etchings of mountains?"

I nodded.

"Okay, but promise no more of this 'me sasquatch, you Jamie' stuff. You have to act normal in public."

I had no idea what she was talking about, so I mumbled my usual answer. "Sorry."

"Let's go. Maybe the pictures will trigger your memory. Follow me."

She headed to the door that led to the orange-haired baldface. I stiffened. "Where are you going?"

"The pictures are in the coffee shop."

"You want me to go out there again?" I asked.

She nodded and headed out, motioning me to follow. I thought about meeting Jamie's mom again and I didn't like the idea. Still, if there was a way home, I had to take the chance. I followed her out of the cave.

The smell of delicious dirt wafted through the air. Before I tried the stuff, the smell made my mouth water; now the smell made me sick to my stomach. I took a quick look around. The mess I'd left had been cleaned up. Baldfaces sat at round tables and sipped a liquid version of the delicious dirt from perma-ice containers. A loud hiss made me jump. The sound came from a large copper container at the back wall of the cave. The baldface with the orange hair stood behind it, watching me. She looked like an older version of Jamie, but with a permanent scowl.

I headed with Jamie to the far end of the cave. She waved at her mother as she walked toward a shelf with a strange box on it.

"Who's your friend?" Jamie's mother asked.

"New kid at school. His name's Barnabas. I'm showing him how he can log into the school website to get his homework assignments."

The orange-haired baldface looked at me. "Have I seen you before?"

I shook my head. Hairy armpits, this baldface scared me. She rolled up the sleeves of her white shirt and pulled a lever on the big copper container. Another hiss. I jumped.

"Remember your promise," Jamie whispered.

"What is this thing?"

"It's an espresso machine," she said. "It makes really strong coffee. You definitely do not want to drink it."

Her mother eyed me. "Are you from Canada?"

I looked at Jamie, who shook her head. "No."

"Ah. Where are you from?"

"The mountains," I answered.

Her mother raised an eyebrow at me, but I didn't know what else to say. Jamie stepped in. "He's from a village in Europe. He told me the name, but don't ask me to say it. I can't pronounce it."

Her mom nodded, then turned to me again. "You're pretty tall to be in grade seven. You look more like you should be in high school."

What was this high school? Something that was tall? Maybe tall baldfaces had to go there. There was much to learn about this strange world.

"Sorry," I mumbled.

"For being tall?" Jamie's mother laughed.

"We have to get to work now," Jamie said, pulling me away from her mother. We sat down at the far end of the coffee shop in front of a flat black board. Square buttons were set across the board's surface like the bumps on a blackberry. She tapped the buttons, then stared at the box mounted on the wall. The box lit up. Bright colours and strange symbols flashed across the board.

"What is this?" I asked.

"It's a computer," Jamie explained. "It's a way to get information very fast."

"When we need to know something, we just talk to each other," I said.

Jamie glared at me. "That's okay when you're right next to each other. With this, I can get information from anywhere in the world."

"Why would you want that?" I asked.

She shrugged. "Because you can."

The baldfaces seemed to want more than they could have in their lives. Like the small white cups they used to sip their delicious dirt. I had seen these cups all over the base of the mountain. Once the baldfaces were done with the cups, they threw them out. I remembered the plates our family used for all our meals. Baldfaces would have only used them once. I shuddered to think how much garbage was piled up in the mall.

Across the screen, weird bird-track symbols showed up along with some strange colourful etchings. My moustache, if I still had one, would have twirled with wonder as I watched the symbols change in the blink of an eye.

"Here's something for you Barnabas," Jamie said. "Gregory Rolands the Third will pay fifty thousand dollars for a sasquatch, dead or alive."

"What are dollars?" I asked.

"It's money," she answered.

I nodded, remembering the word from Dr. Samson. "Why do you need money? Couldn't you just make or gather what you need?"

"We don't have the time to make everything ourselves. It's easier to buy what we want," Jamie explained.

Something on the board caught my eye. I pointed to an etching that looked like a tiny blurry version of me.

"What's that?"

She slid a grey rock across the counter. At the same time, a tiny black arrow flew across the screen.

"This was one of the most popular clips on YouTube last week," Jamie explained.

"What's YouTube?" I asked.

"Videos that people put on the internet."

"What are videos?"

"Moving pictures. Like etchings on a cave wall."

"Ah. What is the internet?"

Jamie sighed. "It's like a storage box to hold all the writing, pictures and movies that people want other people to see."

"Ah, and what are movies?" I asked.

"Never mind," Jamie said, rolling her eyes and huffing. "Just know that this is a way to find your home."

Suddenly, the bird track symbols on the screen disappeared. In their place was a baldface — the one I had played Baldface Chase with; but now she was tiny. What kind of powers did these creatures have that they could shrink and grow? Could she see me? I ducked behind Jamie.

"What are you doing?"

"I don't want her to see me."

"She's not really there, Barnabas. It's an etching, except it can move and talk."

I peeked out from behind Jamie at the baldface on the screen.

The baldface on the screen spoke. "My husband and I were getting in one last camping trip when we saw this huge hairy beast crash out of the forest and come right at us. It was the most hideous thing I've ever seen and I'm a plumber. My husband and I chased after it and we got this shot of it."

The screen changed to show the back of a sasquatch as he lumbered into the woods. I knew those woods.

"That's it," I said, pointing at the etching on the screen. "That's my home."

Jamie tapped the rock and the etching changed to bird track symbols. "I know where your home is. According to the posting, the picture was taken near Harrison."

"Yes, the Hairyson sisters were near," I said.

"What? Who? Harrison. It's a town in B.C.," Jamie explained.

"Hairy armpits! I can go home," I said. "Let's go now."

I got up and headed out of the cave, but Jamie grabbed my arm before I could get two strides.

"You can't walk there, Barnabas. You'd freeze to death before you got out of the city."

"Then how do I get back home?" I asked.

"We could call your dad to come get you."

"Call? How would you call him?"

"On a phone. He must have one of those."

I shook my head.

Jamie sighed. "Look, Barnabas, it was fun for a while to play your sasquatch game, but this is serious. Your family's probably very worried that you're missing. And this Dr. Samson might be worried too."

"No. He's evil."

"Okay, okay. Maybe he is. But we have to tell your parents where you are."

I stiffened as I looked over her shoulder.

"So tell me where I can find them. Please. Barnabas? Can you hear me? Hello?"

I wasn't listening to her. My hair stood straight up as I watched a baldface with a big nose and a black patch over one eye walk toward me. Dr. Samson's hunters had found me.

Chapter Eleven

The baldface with the eye patch stared at a grey box as he wandered past other baldfaces in the mall. He glanced up and looked in my direction, then back at his box. He started to walk toward me.

"Jamie," I whispered. "I think we have to go."

"Why?"

I nodded toward the approaching baldface. He scratched his eye patch and checked the grey box again. Jamie scrunched her eyebrows together, confused.

"Whoa. The eye patch. He's one of the guys you were talking about," she said.

"He's with Dr. Samson."

Jamie looked up at him. "He doesn't look like an orderly."

"He's dangerous."

"I'm sure he just wants to help you."

She started to get up and wave. I grabbed her hand and pulled it down.

"What are you doing? You said you'd help."

"I am, Barnabas. This Dr. Samson is going to give you all the help you need." She walked toward him, but then skidded to a stop. He reached into his hides and checked a black object. It was about the size of his hand, with a pointed end. I had no idea what it was, but Jamie seemed to know, judging by her gasp.

"He's got a gun."

"What's that?"

"I'll explain later. Come with me." She slipped away from the wall, pulling me along.

Too late, the baldface walked into the coffee shop as he looked at the grey box. As he moved closer, the little box made a strange sound. It was like a mother nuthatch chirping at her chicks.

Jamie led me to the back of the cave, waving at her mother. "I'm going to show Barnabas how to do some math problems in the back."

Her mom nodded. Behind us, Dr. Samson's hunter entered the cave. The chirping grew louder and faster. Jamie closed the door behind us.

"How did he find me so fast?" I asked. "Baldfaces must be good trackers."

Jamie shook her head. "This makes no sense at all. You can't be telling the truth, but why does that guy have a gun?"

"I'm not lying, Jamie," I said. "It's all real."

"Shh." She put her ear to the black door and listened. I joined her. On the other side, Jamie's mother talked to the hunter, but I couldn't hear everything.

Her nasally voice drifted through the door. "Some college kid thought it was funny . . . sa squatch . . . .threw up . . . "

" . . . like to talk to him . . . reward . . . " the hunter said.

"How much?"

"What's a reward?" I asked.

Jamie turned to me. "Quiet. I can't hear."

"What do the baldfaces want?" I asked.

She stepped away from the door and grabbed my hand. "We have to go."

"What's wrong?"

"Mom told the guy to talk to me. They're coming."

Jamie headed out the other door. I followed her as she ran into the passageway. In three strides I caught up to her. When we reached the main clearing of the mall, Jamie reached out and stopped me. There were a few baldfaces around, but none looked like the hunters. She motioned me to follow her. We headed toward the stone stairs leading to the lower level.

Around us, baldfaces went in and out of the caves with large, overfull bags. I wondered how much money they used to get the things in their bags and what they did if they didn't have enough money.

Jamie skidded to a stop at the top of the steps. Below us, the bald Dr. Samson handed out grey boxes to two baldface hunters in black hides. They slipped their hands into the hides to check their guns, then split off in different directions, leaving Dr. Samson in the clearing. He checked his grey box, then started toward the stairs leading up to our position. I stiffened, my back hair standing up on end.

"It's him," I said.

"I thought he was your psychiatrist, Barnabas."

"I don't know what that is."

Dr. Samson began to climb the stairs.

"We have to go," I said."

"Oh man, I thought you were just telling some weird story, but it's true. You're . . . you're a sasquatch."

"You said you believed me."

"I was just humoring you until you got the medical help you needed. I thought you were nuts, until I saw all the guns. They're hunting you."

The hairless baldface was halfway up the stairs.

"Yes, and he's going to catch me if we don't go now."

"I'm sorry I didn't believe you earlier, Barnabas," Jamie said. "We can't let them capture you again."

"You'll help me? For real?"

"Yes. Follow me." She started to walk down the stairs. I paused.

"He'll catch me for sure."

"No, we'll walk right past him," Jamie said. "He won't recognize you without your hair."

"Are you sure?"

"You look completely different. Trust me." She started down the stairs.

I followed her, trying not to look at Dr. Samson as he came up, but I couldn't resist glancing his way. The light bounced off his bald top. He stared at the grey box in his hands and didn't even look up. I quickened my pace, but Jamie slowed me down.

As we got closer, the chirping from the box grew faster. Dr. Samson started to look up. His face scrunched with confusion. He glanced back at the grey box. As I walked past Dr. Samson, his grey box let out a long chirp. He looked at my face but said nothing. He shook his grey box.

When we reached the bottom of the steps, I peeked back. Dr. Samson was still shaking his grey box. The other two baldfaces came toward me with their chirping boxes. Above, the baldface with the patch over his eye was making his way toward us. I don't know how, but Dr. Samson's hunters were tracking me. I looked at the shiny white ground, but there were no tracks. I sped up, pulling Jamie behind me. She had to run just to keep up with my loping strides.

She pulled me into a cave that was filled with large shelves and small boxes. The items on the shelves of this bright cave reminded me of all the garbage we found around the baldface shelters near the mountains. Though the smells here were fresher.

"What is this place?"

"This is a grocery store," Jamie said. "I have to get something."

"No time," I said. "We have to get to the mountains," I yipped. Every time I got nervous, my voice went high and yippy like a newborn wolf pup.

"You'll lead Dr. Samson straight to the other sasquatches."

"How?" I asked.

Jamie said. "I think they've tagged you with a locator."

"A what?" I asked as she led me between shelves of foul-smelling baldface goods.

"It's like a tiny bug that sends out an electronic signal. Not a bug like a fly, but a machine. The grey boxes the men have beep faster when they get closer to the locator, which is somewhere on your body."

"I'd notice if there was something attached to me," I said, starting to pat myself from top to bottom.

"Dr. Samson might have planted it inside you."

The thought of a baldface machine swimming inside my body made my remaining hair shrivel. This baldface was a cruel creature.

"Usually, they tag animals on the ears," Jamie said.

"Usually? You mean baldfaces do this to animals too?" I asked.

She nodded. "It's not supposed to hurt them. They're microchips."

"Did you ask the animals? Baldfaces are monsters."

She shook her head. "Not all of us. I think I can do something about the locator."

She stopped at a shelf and pulled out a long blue box with silver bark inside. She rolled out the silver bark and motioned me to bend over. Then she wrapped the shiny bark around my head. The crackle and crinkle sounded like a thousand raccoons running across a meadow of dried leaves.

"This is aluminum foil. It will stop the signal from going out."

"It tickles," I giggled.

"You'll get used to it. Come on." She led me down the path to the front of the cave, where a bored baldface girl stood behind a black boulder. The girl glanced at me for a second then shrugged. Jamie placed the long blue box on the counter and pulled a small blue piece of bark from her top hide. The baldface girl took the bark and handed Jamie a few shiny silver and gold circles.

"What's that?" I asked.

"Money," Jamie said.

So that's what the baldfaces used to get what they wanted. Money didn't look very useful, but the bark and circles looked shiny and pretty.

The baldface looked at me. "Bit late for Halloween, isn't it?"

Jamie pulled me away before I could ask what Halloween was. We rushed through the mall. Some of the shorter baldfaces pointed at my head. The taller ones smiled. One baldface let out a huge laugh.

"Why are they staring at me?" I asked.

"Ignore them."

She pulled me across the mall into another cave that was full of baldface hides. She ran to a silver sapling, which was blooming with black, red, blue and white hides. Jamie motioned me to bend over, as she pulled a brown hide from the sapling and shoved it on my head.

"This is a toque. People wear them in winter. As long as you have it on, no one will notice the aluminum foil around your head. You'll be able to blend in. Now wait here while I pay for this."

She rushed over to the lone baldface in the cave. I took the time to look at the perma-ice mirror beside the rack. My reflection stared back at me. Gone was my beautiful facial hair, replaced with a smooth white face. I was decked out in baldface hides that were too small for me, and now I was wearing a strange black hide and silver bark.

In the mirror, I noticed Dr. Samson. He hadn't spotted me yet. I stepped behind the rack, blending into the baldface store. He stared at his tiny grey box. Beside him was the baldface with the eye patch. I held my breath, waiting for them to walk away. They stopped in front of the cave.

"Dr. Samson, I think the signal died back there," the baldface said.

"You're right, Lucius, but I know the sasquatch is in this mall. I mean how easy is it to hide a seven-foot-tall hairy beast?"

Lucius seemed a strange name for the baldface with the eye patch, but then again everything in the baldface world seemed strange. He nodded at Dr. Samson. "People have seen him, but they all thought it was part of the fur protest stunt."

"We have to find the daughter of the coffee shop owner, and then we'll be able to get some answers."

"How do you know she knows anything?"

Dr. Samson patted Lucius on the arm. "When technology fails, you have to rely on old-fashioned communication. Remember what the security guard said? He said the girl vouched for the sasquatch."

"Do you think she's helping the beast?"

"Yes, and I think I saw the creature on the stairs. They've shaved his face, but they can't hide his height. And once she hears the reward I've put out for his capture, let's see who she wants to help."

"How can you be sure?"

"Lucius, only a fool would say no to the money I'm offering," Dr. Samson said. "Tell your men to be on the look out for a very tall boy and a ginger-haired girl. They'll most likely be traveling together."

The baldfaces split off in opposite directions. I stepped out from behind the sapling, my hair settling down from its porcupine alertness. Jamie tapped my shoulder. I yipped.

"It's me, Barnabas. It's okay, we can go," she said. "We have to find you a place to hide."

"I overheard Dr. Samson. They're not just looking for me. They want to find you too."

I told Jamie what I had heard. She bit her lower lip and scrunched her face as she listened. When I was done, she patted my arm.

"Don't worry, Barnabas. There's no way I'd let that guy capture you."

I grunted.

"I have a plan to get you home. All we have to do is keep you safe for one night."

"What's your plan?"

"We get you a one-way bus ticket to Harrison."

"What's a bus?"

"It's a machine that will take you back to the mountains."

"Like a truck?" I asked.

She nodded. "Once you're there, it'll be up to you to find your family. Do you think you can do that if I get you to the mountains?"

I hugged Jamie. "Yes, yes, yes. That's great. Can we go now?"

"I need to get some money first," she answered. "I don't have enough to buy a ticket today."

I glanced around the mall, to make sure Dr. Samson's tribe wasn't near us. The one called Lucius stood at the far end, while Dr. Samson was walking in the opposite direction.

"How are you going to get the money?"

"Don't worry. I'll take care of it," Jamie said. "Now let's find you a hiding spot."

The hiding place Jamie found me was down the narrow passageway that led to the cramped cave. Instead of stepping in the cramped cave, she led me further down the hall to an even smaller cave. Behind the grey door was a chamber barely large enough for a baldface, let alone me. All I could see was a white shelf and a large mirror on one wall. Beside the shelf sat a strange white stool with a black seat and a thick white back. The cave smelled like dead lilacs.

"What is this place?" I asked, looking at the water in the white stool. "Is this where you go to drink?"

"No, you don't want to drink from the toilet. This is the staff washroom. It's where people go when they have to . . . to . . . never mind. Just get inside and lock the door. If anyone knocks, grunt and moan. In an hour, the mall's going to close and everyone will go home. You'll be safe until morning."

"How will I know when to come out?" I asked, scratching my itchy scalp under the silver bark and black hide.

"You'll know when I come get you," Jamie said. "Now get in there."

I ducked to get through the entrance and stood against the white stone wall. Jamie closed the door. She pointed to the copper knob and told me to push it in once the door was closed. I did as she asked. Then I sat on the squat bench and waited, thinking that I was just a sunrise away from going home.

Chapter Twelve

While I counted the breaths until Jamie's return, I imagined time was a log floating on a river. It could be fast or slow, depending on how much I was enjoying myself. When I had fun, time became white-water rapids, shooting me ahead. When I waited for Hannah or Ruth to stop teasing me, time trickled like a dying brook. Sitting in this cramped cave, time had become a stagnant pond.

A couple of times, baldfaces knocked on the door and scared me so much my hair stood straight up. I let out a grunt and the baldfaces apologized, then they walked away. Eventually the knocking stopped. A thousand breaths later, I heard footsteps moving past the chamber and voices shouting goodbye to one another. Another two hundred breaths later, there was only silence. I didn't know how many breaths it would be before Jamie came back, but I hoped it was soon. I reached under the shirt and twirled the hair on my stomach, which grumbled. Why hadn't Jamie given me some food before she left?

I sniffed the cave, hoping to find something to eat, but the stench of rotten lilacs filled my nose. On the wall in front of the white stool was a roll of white bark. I tapped the soft roll and pulled at a dangling edge. The thin bark reeled off. I lifted the strip to my nose and sniffed. Then I nibbled. It was dry and awful. I spit it out, scraping my tongue. I reached between my legs and scooped some water from the stool and washed out my mouth. I spit out the water. Jamie was right. I shouldn't drink it. Even the water tasted awful. After a few breaths, my stomach stopped grumbling and started growling.

I remembered the trees in the mall. If I could just eat a few leaves, I'd quiet my belly. I pressed my ear at the door to listen for baldfaces. There was no sound. Maybe they were gone. No. Jamie told me this was the safest place. My stomach growled louder than ever. I couldn't ignore my hunger pangs any longer.

I stood up, but my legs wobbled. They tingled like ants were crawling inside them. I propped myself against the stone wall and took deep breaths, trying to shake out the ants. The tingling finally stopped and I could move again. I opened the door and peeked out. No baldfaces. I sniffed the air. No one was near.

I stepped into the passageway and hugged the wall, straining to hear baldface voices. The area was darker than before. The sun must have set. I was used to the night; in fact, I felt safer now that the mall was dark. I crept along the wall, following the scent of the mall trees until I reached the clearing. No one was in the mall. It was empty. If I'd still had a moustache, it would have been twirling with glee. I headed into the clearing and found the steps leading to the lower level and the trees below.

The highest leaves on a tree usually had the tastiest leaves, but the mall trees didn't look anything like the ones in the woods. These trees were sickly skinny compared to the trees I knew. I pulled a branch lower, plucked a leaf and placed it on my tongue. Not as sweet and fresh as the leaves back home, but better than the thin white bark I'd tried to eat earlier. I plucked more leaves off the branches and chewed them into a fragrant mash before swallowing them. I moved from branch to branch and tree to tree, making sure I didn't take too many leaves from one tree. That was the sasquatch way.

When I'd had my fill, I sat down on the ground and gazed at the cave roof. Hanging from the top were large frozen birds. They seemed to be the wrong colour; fiery red, bright blue and pretty pink. These giant birds would never be able to blend in in the forest. Even in this colourful mall, they looked out of place with their outstretched wings. They were trapped in the mall, like the tiny dogs baldfaces kept in cages.

If only I could see past the birds to the night sky. I wanted to play star shapes, but I couldn't see a single star, at least not from inside the mall, and Dad wasn't here. I tried to make shapes using the hanging birds, but the only shape I could make out was a cage, just like the one Dr. Samson had put me in. I gave up on the game.

I leaned against the trunk of the tree and curled up into a ball. I closed my eyes and stared at the inside of my eyelids. The darkness was soon replaced with my memory of my parents. Dad led me to our secret ledge to play another game of star shapes. Mom pulled ticks out of my hair. Then I thought about Hannah chewing on her rat tail of hair.

Grandma Bertha had a saying: "A cave is where you keep your body warm, but your memory is where you keep your heart warm." I tried to remember all the wonderful things about my home and my tribe, but no matter how hard I tried to dream myself back to the mountains I could still feel the cold hard ground of the mall and I could smell the awful baldface odours. They seemed to be everywhere. Their rotten lilac smells, their steaming cups of delicious dirt and their click-clacking footsteps coming closer.

Footsteps? Hairy armpits, one of them was here.

I sat up and scanned the mall. Was it Lucius or Dr. Samson? Or was it a group of hunters? I stayed close to the tree, trying to blend into it. If this were a forest, I'd be invisible, but one tree wasn't going to hide me, especially when my beautiful brown hair was gone. Now that my face was bald, I was like the birds hanging from the cave roof—trapped.

A short baldface figure walked toward me. I held my breath and didn't move a single hair. As the creature came closer, I could smell cougar sweat. I knew that scent. It belonged to the baldface Jamie had talked to earlier. Alvin. He whistled as he walked. He came so close that the smell of his cougar sweat tickled my nose hair and almost made me sneeze. He strolled past me. He hadn't seen me. I was safe. I slid back, bumping into the tree, shaking it.

Alvin spun around and flashed a light across the mall. "Who's there? Mall security! Freeze!"

The beam of light swept the ground in front of me, moving closer. I had to do something. I slid around the trunk of the tree. The beam of light hit the spot where I had been sitting. I stepped back as the light swept the ground toward me.

"Show yourself," he demanded.

I said nothing as I stepped behind the next tree in the row.

"I have a green belt in karate," he said. "So if you're going to try anything, be warned."

I crept behind another tree, avoiding the circle of light as it swept in front of me like a trout zipping back and forth in the water.

Alvin growled. "If someone's there, you'd better come out before I go all *hi-ya* and *keeyahh* on your butt. And if you get me really mad, then I'll be *whap, keeyahh* and *bap* and *yeeee-aaaaaaaaaaa.* You'd better just do yourself a favour and come out."

I couldn't go back any further. I bumped into a perma-ice wall. Through the wall were white-faced baldfaces, frozen like the birds. They wore heavy fur hides. The light flashed in my eyes. I froze and stared out, pretending to be one of the white-faced baldfaces.

"Oh geez, just a mannequin. Ugly one at that," Alvin said. He turned off his light and walked away.

As I listened to his footsteps grow fainter, I relaxed and moved away from the perma-ice wall.

Alvin yelled, "Who's there? Mall security. Freeze!"

I didn't dare breathe. He wasn't looking my way. Instead, he stared in the opposite direction. He waved his arms and legs in the air.

"If someone's there, you'd better come out. I watched all the Bruce Lee and Jackie Chan movies, and I can kick some serious butt. If you don't come out, I'll go all *keeyaah* on you."

The beam of light was aimed at the far end of the cave wall.

"One day, it's going to happen. There's going to be a real break in," he said. "There'll be a gang of them. They'll nab the store owners. Hold them hostage. The head thug will say something evil like, 'You'll never see your families again.' And the hostages will be like, 'Oh no, help us. Someone help us.' And the cops, they'll be all, 'Hey, we're too busy getting doughnuts.' But me, I'll be a man of action. I'll save those store owners. *Hi-ya*! Take that bad guy. *Kee-yah*! Take that, Mr. Thug. And then everyone in the mall will be like, 'Oh, thank you, Alvin, you saved us.' And I'll be, 'It's just part of a day's work. No need to thank me. What's that Mr. Mayor? You want to make me chief of police? I think I just might take that and clean up this city.'"

For some reason, it seemed important that he protect his own kind with his kicking feet. He kept walking down the mall, flashing his light stick and kicking at invisible enemies. I'd want to protect my tribe as well, but not by fighting. I'd rather hide and right now I needed to hide from this baldface.

I crept back to the cramped cave with the white stool. Once safely inside, I curled up beside the white bench and put my head on the floor. There were no hints of my mountain home; no snowcaps on the high mountain tops, no hoots of the screech owls, no sweet scent of pine trees. I wrapped my arms around my bended legs, rocked myself against the hard cold floor and counted my breaths until sleep finally took me over.

Knock, knock, knock. I bolted up and hit my head on the white shelf above me. Hairy armpits, how long had I been sleeping? I had no idea, but the knocking on the door must have meant that Jamie was back. I climbed to my feet and opened the door.

Dr. Samson flashed a thin-lipped smile at me. "Did you miss me?"

CHAPTER THIRTEEN

How could Dr. Samson have found me? As his hunters led me through the mall, my arm hairs felt like they were on fire, matching the fire in my brain as I tried to figure out what had happened. Lucius walked alongside me with his hand on my shirt. On the other side, another baldface held on to my other arm. Ahead of us, Dr. Samson practically skipped as he led us out of the mall. Behind me, I could smell the other hunters. There was no way they were going to let me get away again.

Where was Jamie? Why hadn't she come earlier? We stepped outside into the cold air, which blasted my bare face. I shivered against the cold. The blizzard had left a white blanket across the world.

Dr. Samson headed for the truck, which I recognized instantly as the one I'd ridden in. One of the baldfaces lifted the back wall up. Lucius herded me toward the inside of the truck. Dr. Samson and Lucius joined me inside, while another baldface closed the wall behind us. In the middle of the dim cave was the giant perma-ice chamber. Beside it was Jamie.

"Thank you, young lady, for telling us where your friend was," Dr. Samson said.

My hair shriveled. She had betrayed me! I bared my teeth at her, but she looked away.

"I thought you'd be happy to see your friend, Barnabas," he said.

He knew my name, which meant Jamie had told him everything. I let out a low snarl. Lucius snatched my black toque off my head.

Dr. Samson beamed. "Ah, mystery solved, Lucius. Now we know why the signal died."

Lucius ripped the bits of silver bark off my head. Dr. Samson's hide started to chirp. He reached inside and pulled out the grey box. He pushed a button and the grey box went silent.

"Put him in the cage," Dr. Samson ordered.

I tried to get away, but Lucius grabbed a handful of my arm hair and twisted. I yelped.

"Stop! You're hurting him!" Jamie yelled.

Lucius shoved me inside the perma-ice chamber — the cage — and slammed the perma-ice door closed behind me. The broken wall was now whole again. They must have fixed it while I was gone.

Dr. Samson pounded the wooden wall. The truck lurched forward, sending me off balance. I braced myself against the clear wall, testing it for any weak spots. There were none.

Jamie moved toward me. "I'm sorry, Barnabas."

"Don't talk to me," I said.

She started to say something else, but I covered my ears.

"Please listen to me."

Dr. Samson interrupted, "I wish you could stay and continue this conversation, but I have some hair experiments to run. I trust you left enough hair on the sasquatch for me to test, little girl. Don't worry. He'll be well taken care of. And when I've found a cure for male pattern baldness, I'll return him to his mountain home."

The way Dr. Samson leered at me, I knew he was lying. As I watched him rub his hands together gleefully, a hairy-brained idea took root in my head. It was risky and dangerous, but I was desperate to escape. I tapped on the cage's perma-ice wall.

"It's too bad Jamie cut off my hair. You'll have to wait for a long time for it to grow back. It might slow you down."

"I don't need your beard. The hair on your head will do just fine," he said, his eyes darting back and forth.

"One head of hair is still not a lot. What if you had more sasquatch hair to work with? Would that speed things up?"

He stared at me. "There are more of you?"

"There's a whole tribe of us in the mountains, and I can show you where they live."

"A tribe?" Dr. Samson's lips quivered for a second, then his dark eyes narrowed. He took off his blue hide. "Wait a minute. Why do you suddenly want to help me?"

"Do you think it's any fun living in the mountains and foraging for leaves and pine cones? After I spent one night in the mall and saw all the food and shelter, I wouldn't dream of going back to a cave. I can't wait to bring all my tribe to your world. We'll be much better off here."

Dr. Samson moved closer to the cage.

"Nice try, Barnabas, but I don't believe you."

"At first, I didn't want to come here, because I heard such hair-ible stories, but now that I see all the amazing things you have, this place is really nice," I lied. "I was counting on Jamie to sneak me back to the mountains so I could tell my tribe about the mall. I didn't expect her to betray me."

"I didn't want to," she said.

I ignored her. "Dr. Samson, you can have my whole tribe, but only if you let us live in your world. If all we have to do is give up our hair, why not? Inside the warm mall, we won't need our hair."

He stroked his chin. "Hair recovery is not a precise science. It might take awhile to take a few samples, but I'd be happy to give your tribe a home here. At least until I complete my work. Then you'll be free to live wherever you want."

"By the hair of my chin, I think we have an agreement."

"He'll never let you go, Barnabas. You're too valuable," Jamie warned.

"Why do you care?" I said, snarling.

Dr. Samson pulled her back from the cage and pushed her toward Lucius. Then he approached me.

"Tell me where your tribe is," he demanded through the cage wall.

"You'd just end up getting lost. Why do you think my tribe has been able to hide from you baldfaces for so long? I have to show you our shelter."

"No time like the present. Lucius, tell the driver we're going on a long road trip."

The other baldface nodded. "What about the girl?"

Dr. Samson ran his hand over his bald top. "Can't have her telling mommy or the police about what I'm doing. Let's give Barnabas a traveling companion."

"I won't tell anyone," she said.

He smiled. "Don't worry; once I get all the sasquatches, I'll let you go."

He flashed a smile that made my hair stand on end. I didn't believe him.

He opened the door. "Put the girl in here."

Lucius grabbed Jamie and tossed her inside the cage. I started to come out, but Dr. Samson closed the door in my face.

"No offense, Barnabas, but you smell awful. Better you stay in the cage." He walked away.

I had launched my plan on a still lake and let it float like a leaf on the surface. All it would take was a strong breeze to create a ripple and tip the plan over and sink it. I glanced at the only thing that could create the ill wind: Jamie. I hoped that she wouldn't make any waves.

CHAPTER FOURTEEN

On the journey to the mountains, Jamie and I sat at opposite ends of the perma-ice chamber. I said nothing. I couldn't trust her. I couldn't trust any baldface.

"Listen to me," Jamie whispered. "They won't ever let your tribe go."

I turned away from her in time to see Dr. Samson approaching with his snip-snaps. He opened the cage.

"Just need a sample, Barnabas. It won't hurt." He smiled.

I backed away from him until I was up against the perma-ice wall beside Jamie. He walked closer with the silver snip-snaps. I started to whimper and curl up into a ball.

Jamie raised a hand. "You're going to hurt him. If you want a hair sample, give me the scissors."

He hesitated, glanced at me and then handed the snip-snaps, the scissors, to her. She leaned forward, but I pushed back, trying to get away from her. I pressed against the corner. No place to go. I cringed as she came nearer, but she shushed me. Gently, she ran a hand through the back of my hair and snipped off a lock of my hair. She handed the hair and the scissors to Dr. Samson.

"You'd make a good lab assistant." He left the cage and closed the door behind him.

I slid away from Jamie and jammed myself into the corner. "Stay away from me."

"Let me explain, Barnabas," she said.

I shook my head.

"I didn't want to tell him anything, but Dr. Samson threatened me."

"You just wanted the reward money."

"Please believe me. I was trying to protect my mom."

"Baldfaces are all the same," I whispered. "That's why we hide from your kind."

"No, I'm not like the others. Dr. Samson said he'd shut down my mom's coffee shop forever."

I raised an eyebrow. Then I glanced at Dr. Samson, who was watching us through the cage's perma-ice wall. He cocked his head to the side.

"Is it true what Jamie said?" I asked.

He nodded. "Yes. I'd shut down the shop for health code violations. Imagine the horror of keeping a live animal in the store. I'm sure the health inspectors would find enough of Barnabas' hair to back up my accusation."

"The coffee shop is my mom's life," Jamie explained. "I couldn't let anything happen to it. You understand, don't you?"

I turned my back on her, brought my knees up to my chest and crossed my hairy arms around them. She sat on the opposite end of the cage, but I refused to look at her. We didn't speak to each other for the rest of the journey. I don't know how many breaths passed, but we were in the cage long enough for my limbs to get stiff and for my stomach to growl again.

At long last, the truck stopped moving. Dr. Samson stood up while Lucius picked up a boom stick. He ran his hand along the smooth black end, hooked it around a brown strap and slung the boom stick over his shoulder.

"We're in the mountains," Dr. Samson said. "Time to find your tribe."

He opened the perma-ice door. Soon I could spring my plan into action, but not just yet. When the baldfaces opened the back wall to the truck, I'd vault outside and outrun them just as I had the first time. There was no way they could catch me once I hit the ground running.

Dr. Samson ordered Lucius, "Get some rope. Tie the girl to the sasquatch."

"Why?" I asked.

"In case you get any ideas about running, I thought we'd weigh you down."

Hairy armpits, this wasn't part of the plan. Lucius tied a yellow vine around my wrist and attached the other end to Jamie's wrist. The vine cut into my skin and made it burn, but I gritted my teeth against the pain.

"The sasquatch is secure," Lucius shouted. "Open the door."

The back door slid up. Outside were the other two baldfaces, armed with boom sticks, but I didn't care. My nose picked up scent of fir trees and earthy soil. Home.

"What are you waiting for?" Dr. Samson asked. "Time is money."

"This way," I mumbled.

Jamie and I stepped out of the truck. She dragged her feet, unable to keep up with my long strides. I had to shorten my steps to let her keep up. There was no escaping as long as she was tied to me.

"It's down this trail," I said, leading the baldfaces into the woods. I didn't know if Mom had moved the tribe yet, so I'd better not take any chances. I decided to lead the hunters away from the caves. I searched the area for anything that might help me out of this mess.

Jamie stumbled beside me as I led everyone to the steepest sections of the mountain. Behind us, the baldfaces scrambled along the slope and started to fall behind. Dr. Samson huffed and puffed, but Lucius was barely winded. I picked up the pace, dragging Jamie with me. This was a real game of Baldface Chase, except it was a game I couldn't lose.

"You're sure you know where you're going?" Dr. Samson asked, panting.

I nodded. "If it were easy to get to our home, you baldfaces would have found us a long time ago."

Jamie fell to the rocky ground and let out a cry. "My knee. Ow."

"Keep going," Lucius ordered.

I pulled her to her feet and continued walking. I stepped over fallen trees and pushed higher up the slope and into the forest. I could easily blend in, but only if I broke free from Jamie. I grabbed the yellow vine around my wrist. The knots were tight and there was no way I could slip out of the bonds easily. I might be able to bite through them, but not before a baldface shot me. If I was going to escape, I'd have to drag her with me.

I glanced back at Dr. Samson and his tribe. They were lagging behind, ducking under the fir tree branches and spitting out pine needles. As we walked, one of Grandma Bertha's sayings popped into my head: a bear is your worst enemy, until you get him up a tree; then he's the tree's problem. I smiled. I knew what I had to do. I slowed down, so the baldfaces moved closer to me.

"Are we there yet?" Dr. Samson whined.

"No. Stay close to me," I said. "Sasquatches have very good sense of smell. If you move too far away, my scent won't cover up your baldface stink."

While this was true, I wanted the baldfaces herded together for another reason. I grabbed Jamie's arm with one hand and a low hanging branch with the other. I sped up as I ducked low.

"What's he doing?" yelled Lucius. "Look out — "

His warning came too late. I let go of the branch. It whipped Dr. Samson in the face, knocking him back. He stumbled and fell to the ground. The others rushed to his side.

I threw Jamie over my shoulder and ran as fast as I could up the mountain. She screamed as she bounced up and down on my knobby shoulder, but I ignored her shouts. I couldn't run as fast with her over my shoulder, but I only needed to get far enough away to give myself time to bite through the vine.

Behind us, Lucius barked, "Shoot him. Take him down."

Tiny arrows thwocked into the trees beside us. I dodged through the trees. Jamie cried in pain as she bounced on my shoulder, but I ignored her as I rushed ahead through the forest. Once we were far enough from the hunters, I slowed down and she stopped yelling.

Suddenly, a huge web hoisted us up in the air.

"Aiyee!" Jamie screamed.

I struggled against the web. The baldfaces had left their traps behind! I felt stupid for not paying closer attention to where I was going. Jamie squirmed in the black web, which caused us to swing in the air. She called for help.

"Quiet! Dr. Samson will hear you."

"Let me out of here! I'm scared of heights."

"Shh. You'll give us away," I said.

I clamped a hand over Jamie's mouth. The web creaked as it swung back and forth and then stopped altogether. I could hear the baldfaces approaching. The crunch of dried leaves filled the air along with the mutterings of Dr. Samson. Below us, the baldfaces trudged through the woods. Lucius stared at the trail, while the other two baldfaces helped Dr. Samson walk.

Lucius stopped under us and surveyed the trail. "Their footprints are gone."

Dr. Samson said, "Maybe they doubled back."

"No. They're here. I can sense them." He scanned the area. If he looked up, we were done for.

Suddenly, a sharp crack sounded from off to the right. Lucius bounded after it, followed by the hunters. Dr. Samson followed, yelling "Let's go back to the truck and get the tracking devices. We'll find the beast in no time."

Once they were gone, I let go of Jamie's mouth. "Are you going to stay quiet?"

She nodded. I bit at the bonds around my wrist. They tasted like pine cones dipped in swamp water. I kept chewing until I was free.

"Once they get the tracking devices, they'll find you," she said.

I forgot about the thing they'd planted in me. If I didn't get out of the net now, Dr. Samson would capture me again. I bit down on a web strand and started to chew as fast as I could. Jamie looked down.

"Is this the best idea?" she asked.

I ignored her. After a few bites, the strands snapped in half. A good sign. I chewed at the other strands of the web, trying to snap enough of them to make a hole in the web. The sunlight faded as I worked into the twilight.

Jamie said, "What happens when you break through the net?"

Snap. The last strand snapped off and the net gave way under our weight. We plummeted to the ground. She screamed. I landed on my back and Jamie plopped on top of my stomach, knocking the wind out of me. My chest hurt, but I could still move. I pushed Jamie away and sniffed the air. No sign of Dr. Samson or the other baldfaces.

"Ow," Jamie said. "That's the last time I want to do something like that."

"Shh," I said. "I smell something." The distinct smell of delicious dirt greeted my nose. I crawled across the ground. Some baldface had sprinkled delicious dirt all over the area.

"Smell this," I said, holding a clump of dirt and delicious dirt.

"Coffee," Jamie said.

"Why would baldfaces leave this here?"

"Maybe it's like bait. You seemed to enjoy the coffee back at my mom's shop."

"Yes, but the baldfaces don't know that," I said. How did they know that delicious dirt would attract a sasquatch? Unless they were hunting a certain rat-tailed sasquatch and her bratty sister? I beamed. Hannah and Ruth had to still be around, which meant my tribe was close by, too.

The trick was how to find them. There was only one place I knew to go. Jamie and I moved down the mountain toward the place where the sisters had played Baldface Chase. At the edge of the woods, I squatted and peered around the clearing. There were many trucks in the area and baldfaces around fires. One of them must have set the trap that caught us. Worried she would give me away, I started to put my hand over her mouth.

Jamie stopped me and whispered, "You don't have to do that, Barnabas. I want to help you."

"Why should I believe you?"

"I could have screamed in the net. After I saw what Dr. Samson was doing with your hair, I knew he was never going to let you go. That's not right. I want to help you."

"The best thing you can do is go to those baldfaces so I don't have to worry about you."

"I won't leave you, Barnabas. I'll help you get the tracker out of your ear."

"Go, Jamie."

She didn't budge, but the baldfaces did. They scrambled out of their seats, grabbed their boom sticks and pointed them into the woods, but they weren't pointing at us. They were pointing toward another section of woods. I could hear something crashing through the forest. I couldn't see who was making the noise, but I smelled Hannah's musky scent.

"I think I found who I was looking for."

"Who?"

"The one who led Dr. Samson and his hunters away earlier."

The baldfaces rushed into the woods, but after a few breaths, they returned with nothing to show for their efforts. I grabbed Jamie and led her into the woods, following my nose. Soon the woods were silent again. I strode ahead a few hundred strides, sure that I was on the right track.

Suddenly a dark shape rushed at Jamie and knocked her to the ground. Then the figure tackled me. I landed on my back with Hannah on top of my chest.

"Hairy Armpits! Get off me," I hissed.

Hannah growled. "Get out of the woods."

"It's me," I yelped. "Hannah, it's me."

She ripped off a nearby branch and raised it over her head.

"How do you know my name?"

"It's me. Barnabas. Barnabas Bigfoot," I said. "Don't you recognize me?"

Behind me, Jamie let out a groan as she tried to climb to her feet. Hannah knocked her down with the branch. Then she shoved the branch against my bare neck and put her weight on it.

"You're a baldface liar," she said.

"Look at me, Hannah. It's me."

"You're wearing clothes and your hair's gone," Jamie moaned. "She thinks you're human."

"Smell me!" I ripped away the top hide and flashed my armpit at Hannah.

She sniffed the air, then moved closer to my armpit and got a good whiff. "Yummy. You smell like delicious dirt, and . . . and . . . sweet cherries. It *is* you, Barnabas."

She rolled off me, letting me sit up. "We thought you were gone forever. What happened to you?"

"No time to explain now," I said, as I tore off the rest of the hides. "We're in danger."

Hannah refused to look away from my face. "What happened to your beard?"

"The only way to blend in with the baldfaces was to look like them."

"You mean like that ugly thing?" Ruth pointed at Jamie.

"She's a friend," I said. "There's a baldface in the woods who is trying to capture sasquatches."

Hannah nodded. "So is every other baldface here. I've been trying to distract them so Dogger Dogwood can lead the tribe out of the mountains."

"Dogger Dogwood? What about my mom?" I asked.

Hannah looked down at her gigantic feet. "No one's heard from the scouting party for days. Your dad said it'd take them time to find a new shelter for all of us, but Dogger Dogwood said the baldfaces were getting too close to our caves and we had to leave right away. Most of the tribe agreed with Dogger Dogwood."

"Everyone left?" I asked.

She shook her head. "Your dad, my parents, Ruth and Yolanda Yeti's clan stayed behind to wait for the scouting party and to keep the baldfaces from tracking the tribe. We've been taking turns coming down here to play Baldface Chase so they stay down here. Sometimes it works; sometimes, it doesn't. They've set traps everywhere and they keep moving closer to the caves. You should head home, Barnabas. Your dad's been worried ever since you were captured."

As much as I wanted to see Dad, I knew I couldn't go up as long as Dr. Samson was tracking me. I had to get rid of the tracker he had planted inside me. "Not yet," I said.

"Why not?"

"There's something I have to do."

Jamie crept over to us. "I don't mean to break up this happy reunion, but we'd better get out of here. Dr. Samson and his men could be anywhere."

I sniffed the air. Sure enough, I smelled Dr. Samson's hunters. They were about fifty strides away and getting closer. As long as they could track me, I could never join the sasquatch tribe. I started to walk away. Hannah reached out and stopped me.

"Not that way. The baldfaces set traps down that path. The kind that bite into paws. I had to help a raccoon out of one of these things two sunsets ago."

Baldfaces everywhere. Traps everywhere. This used to be a peaceful mountain. Suddenly, a fly of an idea buzzed across my mind.

"Hannah, are there any traps like the web we first saw?" I asked.

She nodded. "About two hundred strides up the mountain. I collected all the delicious dirt, but the web is still there."

"Okay. Take Jamie up there," I instructed.

"What are you going to do, Barnabas?" Jamie asked.

"I'm going to give Dr. Samson what he wants," I answered. "Hannah, when you hear me get close, give me a whistle so I know where the trap is. If we're lucky, this will work."

Hannah nodded. "Come on, baldface. Let's go. And stay downwind of me. You stink."

"You're no bed of roses either," Jamie said as she followed Hannah up the mountain.

I waited until they were a hundred strides away, and then I started to crash through the woods, smacking my hands against the trees and whooping. I growled and howled, until I heard baldface voices shouting. In the dark, I'd have a great advantage over the baldfaces. I could smell them from a thousand strides away.

Dr. Samson yelled. "The tracker's pinpointed him, Lucius. He's fifty metres to your left."

Lucius yelled. "Break out the night scopes."

What were night scopes?

A baldface shouted, "I see the target."

How? It was night. Even with the moonlight, I would have been nearly invisible to the baldfaces. *Thwock. Thwock. Thwock.* Little arrows hit the tree beside me. The baldfaces could see me. I scrambled away. The little arrows flew around me as Dr. Samson's tribe members gave chase. They spread out through the woods, forcing me to run in one direction, and that direction was away from Hannah and Jamie. Another arrow whizzed past my head when I tried to turn back up the mountain. I tried again, but the baldfaces kept firing at me. I had to turn back down the mountain.

As I hurtled through the woods, I moved in the direction of the baldface camp. All those hunters made my hair stand on end. Dr. Samson was going to get me, but at least Jamie would be safe, and Hannah could go back to the tribe and tell them that I was alive. Another arrow narrowly missed my head and splashed in the swamp water just beyond the trees.

Swamp? Hairy armpits! Perfect.

"Ow! That hurt!" I screamed, lying.

Dr. Samson yelled. "Close in on the sasquatch! Move fast."

I crashed through the woods toward the swamp. My foot-hides went into the muck, which was now freezing cold. I waded through the stuff, standing up as tall as I could.

Lucius yelled, "Got him. This way."

He and two hunters ran after me with their boom sticks raised. I kept moving forward. I had to lure them a few strides further. Just a little more.

"Ahhh!" yelled a baldface. "There's a bog here. Careful."

Perfect. I lowered myself into the murky water and disappeared from their view.

"He's gone," cried the other one.

"No, the tracker says he's near," Dr. Samson said.

I waded through the swamp until I was next to two of the baldfaces. I reached up and pulled them both down into the muck. They dropped their boom sticks in the water. As they tried to stand up and find their boom sticks, I slipped away. I peered up and saw Lucius sweeping his boom stick back and forth. Slowly, I approached him.

At the edge of the swamp, Dr. Samson yelled. "He's moving closer. He's coming to you. He's coming."

Before Lucius could react, I grabbed his legs and pulled.

"Glub!" He fell face-first into the muddy swamp. His boom stick went flying into the water.

I smiled as I glided away from the baldfaces in the swamp. They were covered in mud. I headed for Dr. Samson, but I stopped when I saw him aiming at boom stick at the water in front of me.

"I see you on my tracker, Barnabas. You might as well come out and make this easier on yourself."

I slid to the right. He swung the boom stick in my direction. He could see me on the tracker. I had no choice but to stand up.

"Nice try, Barnabas. I have to admit you sasquatches are much more clever than I gave you credit for. I underestimated you. I won't do that again. Now if you'll be so kind as to stand still so I can hit you with the tranquilizer. One sasquatch is better than none."

He raised his long boom stick. Suddenly he screamed as the boom stick and grey box went flying out of his hands and he splashed into the swamp. Behind him stood Jamie.

She motioned for me to join her. I made a beeline for her, stepping on Dr. Samson as he tried to get up. Like his tribe members, he was covered in brown muck. Perfect.

I grabbed Jamie and led her to the baldface camp.

As we ran, she shouted, "We knew something was wrong when you didn't follow us. I figured Dr. Samson needed a little swim in the swamp, so I gave him a push."

I smiled. "Great."

"Where's Hannah?"

"Halfway up the mountain. Some hunters were in the area. She's trying to lead them away."

"I'll find her."

"Barnabas, you can't stay here. You have to find a new home far away from here. Do you understand? The people . . . the baldfaces won't stop looking for you. Especially not Dr. Samson. He'll never let you see your family again."

"Hold your hair," I said. "That reminds me of something."

"What?"

"Alvin said something in the mall."

Jamie scrunched her face, confused. "Why are you thinking of Alvin? He's just a whack job with a badge."

"I have an idea," I said.

"What?"

Before I could answer, I heard the baldfaces crashing through the woods. I looked back and saw Dr. Samson and his tribe stumbling toward us. I let them get closer. Without their boom sticks, I didn't have to rush. When they were a few strides away, I grabbed Jamie and ran through the woods toward the baldface campsite.

As we ran, I asked Jamie, "You baldfaces care about families, don't you?"

She nodded. "Yes, but I won't leave you alone against Dr. Samson."

I smiled. "No, you're going to help capture him."

Jamie scrunched her face. "What? How?"

"Go to the baldfaces in the camp. Tell them you're in trouble and Dr. Samson is after you."

"What?"

"Tell them he's been hunting you. That he won't let you see your family."

She beamed. "Yes, of course, I get it. That's a brilliant idea. We'll make the men think Dr. Samson is trying to hurt me."

"Yes. Hurry, Jamie."

The hunters were getting closer. She hugged me. "I'm sorry I turned you in."

"I'd do anything to protect my parents too. It's all right. I'm home now."

I let go of Jamie and slipped into the woods, slid next to a wide tree and blended into the dark forest. Meanwhile, Jamie crashed through the forest and led the baldfaces away from me.

Dr. Samson yelled, "I hear him. After him. This way."

The baldfaces rushed past me as they chased after Jamie. I couldn't leave her just yet. Not until I knew she was safe. I followed Dr. Samson and his hunters as they chased her. She ran out of the woods and into the clearing where the other baldfaces were gathered.

Jamie screamed, "Help me! Someone's trying to kidnap me. Help!"

She ran to the campfire, just as Dr. Samson and hunters ran into the clearing. They skidded to a stop when they saw the group of baldfaces around Jamie.

She yelled, "There are the kidnappers!"

The baldface hunters let out a collective whoop and charged. I didn't stick around to see what happened next, but I was pretty sure Dr. Samson wasn't going to be coming after me tonight. We had a head start. I glanced back at the campfire. Jamie looked at the woods, waving at me. I waved back and then I slipped into the woods to find my tribe.

Chapter Fifteen

As I ran up the slope of the mountain, the familiar smells greeted me. I imagined what my dad would do when he saw me. I imagined his moustache curling with glee as I ran into his big, hairy arms. I imagined him not caring about my bald face. We'd find our favourite ledge and play star shapes until I fell asleep and he'd cradle my head in his lap and tell me everything would be okay.

But when I reached my cave home, there was no happy scene. Instead there was a hairy tangle. Branches and rocks were scattered everywhere like there had been a struggle here. Two baldfaces stood in the middle of our camp area.

One of them shouted at the other, "They've scattered everywhere. Signal the main party to scour the mountain."

"I'm not going anywhere!" That voice belonged to my dad. He stood in front of the cave entrance, alone. "Come and get me."

The baldfaces raised their boom sticks and advanced on my dad. He turned and scrambled, not into the cave but up the mountain. He was moving to the rocky cliff where we played star shapes. He was playing Baldface Chase to give the other sasquatches enough time to get away.

One of the baldfaces yelled. "We've got this one. He's got no place to go but up."

They chased after my dad. I ran after them, stopping at the cave to pick up a couple of large stones. If there was a chance to help my dad, I'd use the stones. The moonlight gave me all the light I needed to see. Unfortunately, it also gave the baldfaces the light they needed to track my dad. He stood in front of the wide gap before the rock shelf where we played star shapes. There was nowhere else to go. He jumped over the wide gap and landed on the rocky ledge.

"He's trapped," one of the baldfaces yelled. "Take him down."

The other baldface raised his boom stick.

"No!" I yelled.

I hurled one of the stones at the baldface. It hit him in the back of the head and knocked him to the ground, but I was too late. The boom stick went off.

Dad let out a yelp. I couldn't see, but I knew that sound meant he'd been hit by one of the little arrows. The other baldface raised his boom stick and fired. Dad yelped again. I hurled my second stone at the baldface and hit him on the side of the head. He fell to the ground beside the first hunter.

"Dad," I yelled, rushing up the mountain.

"Barnabas? Barnabas! Is that you?"

"Yes, I'm coming. Just sit down. You're going to get sleepy soon."

His legs started to wobble. "I knew you'd find a way home. I knew it."

"Sit down!"

He didn't listen. He stepped back and took a run at the wide gap. His legs gave way, and instead of jumping over the gap, he fell into it. In the blink of an eye, he was gone.

"Dad!!!"

I started to run toward the gap, but hairy hands grabbed me from behind. It was Hannah and her sister.

"No, Barnabas!" she yelled. "It's too dangerous."

"The baldfaces are getting up, and there are more coming," Ruth said.

"I have to save my dad!" I screamed.

"It's too late," Hannah said.

The two sisters were too strong for me. They pulled me away. As much as I struggled, I couldn't get away. Dad would have grabbed on to the ledge, I thought. I yelled at the Hairysons, "Let me go. Dad needs my help."

"You can't help him now," Ruth argued.

"They hit him with the arrows that'll make him sleep. I have to go!"

"Barnabas, he fell off the mountain," Hannah said. "He's gone. I'm sorry, but we can't lose you too."

I shook my head. "Let me go."

Around us, the sounds of the baldfaces were everywhere. They had found our home. The sisters dragged me into the woods as the baldfaces swarmed all over my home. I looked back at rocky ledge where my dad and I had played star shapes. My chest felt like someone had stabbed a burning branch into it. I wanted to play star shapes one more time with my dad. I wanted to feel his hairy arms around me, but that was never going to happen. Everything had changed, and it was my fault.

As we headed down the slope, I took one last look at my mountain home. Nothing was ever going to be the same again.

Novelist, playwright, television writer, and radio humorist, MARTY CHAN has been entertaining audiences across Canada for over fifteen years. His first children's novel, *The Mystery of the Frozen Brains*, won the 2005 City of Edmonton Book Prize. The sequel, *The Mystery of the Graffiti Ghoul*, won the 2008 Diamond Willow Award. He was the story editor on the Gemini Award-winning kids' series *Incredible Story Studio*, and he wrote "The Orange Seed Myth", a half-hour television program that won the Gold Medal for Best Children's Television Pilot at the Charleston World Television Festival. His stage play, *Mom, Dad, I'm Living with a White Girl,* has been produced across Canada as well as Off Broadway in New York. Chan lives in Edmonton, AB.